To the Point

Stories and Poems

To the Point

Stories and Poems

LOUISE SEARL

Published by Wordzworth
www.wordzworth.com

Contents

Be Careful What You Wish For

Shanna, the Amur leopard, paced up and down obsessively. It was nearly feeding time and she knew the keeper would soon appear. It was dark, the visitors had all left hours ago. There had been some tasty looking children in the crowd today, but try as she might she could never reach them through the thick plate glass of the prison which was home.

She had been born in captivity, but her mother had told her stories about the lives of their forbears who had lived in the wild. She knew that there are few Amur leopards left in the forests and mountains of China and Russia, and her dearest wish was to be there herself. She wanted to run in the huge open spaces, to hunt her own food and never again see the faces of human visitors, desperate for a glimpse of her agility, and the sound of her distinctive rasping bark.

Shanna was sick of her enclosure. She was sick of the sight of the three trees within the enclosure. She was sick of the sight and sound of the visitors. She was sick of the routine. She longed for release from captivity. She longed for excitement and danger, for her life to be her own.

One day she was woken and found herself being herded into a box on wheels. Before she knew what was happening she was travelling along a bumpy road. The zoo had been left far behind. Through the bars of the wagon she could see fields, trees, hills and sometimes people and their houses. Eventually there appeared huge machines with wings like birds, nestling on the ground. The wagon stopped and she was let into a small enclosure and sedated. She slept all through the flight. The next thing she was aware of was being released into a large grassy area. It was a bit like the zoo she had left, but there were no gawping crowds. The she realised there was no keeper coming in every night with meat. Instead, every evening she was let out into a vast wild area where there were other animals she could eat if she could catch them. She was happy in that half-way house between captivity and freedom. She soon became a skilled hunter and caught enough prey to assuage her hunger. She found the water holes where she could both drink and stalk unwary victims. She adapted quickly to her new surroundings.

The keepers had been watching Shanna. They noticed how quickly she learned to hunt. She was part of a programme whereby animals raised in captivity are gradually returned to their natural habitats to breed. They saw that she was capable of surviving in the wild. They were about to grant her dearest wish.

Once more she was transported to an airfield. When she saw the airfield she wondered what was happening now. Was she on her way back to the zoo? No! She was sedated and put aboard the aircraft which would take her far far away to Russia, to her homeland. When she awoke after the long flight she knew instinctively she had reached home. She looked around her. She sniffed the air, she knew this was where she belonged. At last she was free.

She set off to explore this wonderful paradise. She found a group of deer grazing and soon singled one out, a little apart from the rest. Later she settled in a leafy hollow, aware that her coat, thickening up now for the winter, would act as camouflage. She knew that she must rely on her own wits and survival instinct. She was in her own country, home at last.

Leopard skin coats fetch a good price overseas. The skin of the Amur leopard is particularly prized. Shanna was being watched. Every day she slept in sheltered spots. Every evening she set out to catch her food. She delighted in the space around her and in the many smells and sounds of the bush. Sometimes she picked up the scent of humans, still familiar to her from her years in the zoo. Sometimes she noticed trails in the undergrowth which had been made by man. Her instinct was to avoid such areas.

The season changed. It became colder and prey was harder to find. Occasionally, when she was very hungry and had had no success in hunting, she remembered how her keeper used to bring her ration of fresh meat every evening. But then she also remembered being confined in a small space, and how she was stared at by human beings every day. Here she was free.

Spring was on the way. Shanna met a male Amur leopard and they mated. She bore four beautiful cubs. She was a good mother, spending hours feeding her babies and later hunting tirelessly for fresh meat to take back to where her cubs awaited her return. One particular day when she had failed to catch any food, she followed the track in the undergrowth which smelt of humans. Suddenly a set of metal teeth closed round one of her legs. Searing pain swept through her body. She was trapped. The more she struggled the tighter became the grip on her leg. As Shanna lay for hours, bleeding, panting and twitching with pain, she thought of her hungry and vulnerable cubs awaiting her return, and she realised that although she would never have turned down the chance of freedom, there was a price to pay. And then she died.

The Skeleton in the Cupboard

The elderly couple next door at Number 43 were good neighbours. Cyril was a kindly, dapper white-haired gentleman but it was Mavis who wore the trousers. I often heard her issuing orders to Cyril as he laboured in the garden or as they left their house on the way to the shops.

Formidable is the word that best describes Mavis. Her upright demeanour and severe expression indicated someone never to be contradicted. Her grey hair was tidily arranged in a bun, her clothes, in colours covering the whole spectrum between brown and beige, were plain and sensible. She did not suffer fools gladly. Sometimes it seemed she barely suffered Cyril.

The only time that Mavis relaxed was when their daughter, and only child, Pauline came to see them. In Mavis's eyes Pauline could do no wrong. She was married to Fred, tolerated by Mavis for the sake of her daughter. Pauline, with her bleached hair and generously applied fake tan, was in no way a chip off the old block. Mavis and Cyril's old fashioned standards of make-do and mend, and never spending money without due care and attention, had not been inherited by Pauline.

One day on my way home from work I was waylaid by Cyril, clearly upset.

'Just thought I should let you know, we've had some bad news. It's Mavis…' Tears welled up in the old man's eyes.

'Oh Cyril, what's happened?'

'I don't suppose you knew she's been going for tests at the hospital? Today they told us she only has a few months left…'

I had noticed she had aged lately, but had not realised it was anything serious. I offered to help in any way I could. There's really no adequate response to such news. Cyril thanked me and promised to let me know if they needed help. Mavis went downhill very rapidly. Occasionally I did bits of shopping or collected prescriptions for them. I took to popping in for a few minutes after work or at weekends, and was shocked to see how fast Mavis changed from a force of nature to a frail old lady. Her one pleasure was visits from Pauline, which, I was pleased to see, increased in frequency.

Mavis died one cold morning in November. The very next week, even before the funeral, I noticed a removal van outside the house as I left for work. Surely Cyril was not moving away? I found out soon enough what had happened. Pauline and Fred had spotted the opportunity of free accommodation and had moved in. They had somewhat tactlessly put their house on the market while Mavis was still alive. It was sold for a good price. Pauline spoke to me over the garden fence the following weekend.

'Mum would have wanted us to look after poor Dad. He's absolutely useless in the kitchen and I can't bear to think of him having to do everything for himself at his age. Me and Fred will take care of him.' I doubted the truth of that statement as I knew that Cyril was actually a pretty good cook and was accustomed to managing all the household chores, albeit directed by Mavis.

Number 43 suddenly acquired a new kitchen, a conservatory, double glazing and a block-paved drive. Pauline and Fred were able to indulge themselves in three expensive foreign holidays as well as a giant wall-mounted television, a new car, a wet room and frequent online shopping deliveries.

Poor Cyril seemed to shrink into himself. He stopped going to the shops as Pauline did the grocery shopping online and he no longer pottered in the garden as Pauline and Fred had the whole area paved over. It was only a matter of time until he too became ill. His mind started wandering and he showed signs of dementia. Pauline remarked that he kept talking about someone called Verity. She thought Verity might have been a little girl Cyril knew as a child. I'm not sure how much caring he received from Pauline. She did say they couldn't afford a carer for him, which I thought was strange. True, the deliveries of parcels seemed to have tailed off. Surely they could not have spent all the money from the sale of their house already?

Oh yes they could. And oh yes they had. They were not too bothered, for surely when Cyril died Pauline would inherit the house? Of course poor Cyril did indeed die. However, he had had one last trick up his sleeve. After Pauline and Fred moved in, and before succumbing to his final illness, Cyril had re-written his will. He deleted Pauline's name and left Number 43 to another daughter, Verity, born before he married Mavis. He had never told Mavis or Pauline about her existence. Verity was his skeleton in the cupboard. Pauline should not have counted her chickens before they hatched!

The Last Day

I wake up. I kick my legs and stretch my arms as widely as I can. I don't know if I'm imagining it but I don't seem able to move around much any more. They played that music at me again before my sleep. I heard the Daddy say:

'Listen to this lovely Mozart, Baby. It's helping to develop your brain.' Really? Later the Mummy said:

'Not long until we see you, Baby. Any day now!' I wonder what she means. I can't see anything, my eyes won't open.

I've been in here as long as I can remember. It's warm and quiet, although not quite as comfy as it was because of the space problem. There is a long cord attached to my body. When I'm thirsty I drink amniotic fluid. Sometimes I hear a horrible barking sound, and usually the Mummy or the Daddy say:

'Quiet Fido, you'll frighten the baby.'

As well as hearing the Mummy and the Daddy I can often hear a very high voice and the Mummy and the Daddy talk to it as well. It's called the Sophie. Other voices have said to the Sophie:

'Are you going to help Mummy and Daddy look after the baby when he arrives?' And 'It'll be lovely for you, Sophie, having a little brother to play with.' The Sophie usually says something along the lines of:

'I don't want a baby in my house. I want a kitten,' which the Daddy and the Mummy choose to ignore. One day the Sophie spoke to me herself:

'You've got my old cot. And my baby blankets and a new teddy. But I've got the big bedroom, and you aren't allowed in, so there.' Of course I didn't have a clue what she was talking about but it didn't sound friendly. The Mummy told her not to be unkind.

I have cut down on the kicking. I need to rest. I doze off for a long time.

I wake up to find something really strange and new has started happening. The walls are moving in, squeezing me along, head first through a tight tube. It's quite tiring. When the walls move in I move along. I only stop when the walls go out a bit. I can't sleep. It's happening slowly in spurts of moving and resting. I can't move my arms or my legs away from my body. Now my head is stuck! What's going on? I feel the Mummy's hands checking where I am. She often does that. She says to the Daddy:

'The baby's head's engaged and he's stopped moving. I'm having a few twinges and I've had a show. I think I'm really in labour at last! Today is the actual due date.' The Daddy says:

'I'll ring the office and tell them I'm not coming in. Then I'll take Sophie round to your mum's. You should try and rest while you can.' I doze off again.

I can hear the Mummy and the Daddy but sometimes the Daddy goes away and comes back later. I don't think I can go back to where I was. I'm being propelled to an unknown destination.

The Mummy doesn't sound like herself at all. She's making funny noises. There are other people there too. One is something called a doctor. She puts her hand up the tube I'm in and moves it around. Quite a weird feeling! She reports:

'The baby is not in distress and he's in a good position, You are fully dilated, remember to take deep breaths. I'll leave you with the midwife now.' The midwife tells the Mummy to take gas and air when she feels a contraction coming. This is a very strange day. I have a feeling it's the start of something new and exciting. What will happen next? I'm now making very slow progress. Then I stop. Now the Mummy has started panting.

'Just one more push. I can see his head. Baby's nearly here'. Suddenly I can't go any further even though the walls are squeezing me. There's something pulling round my neck. Oh dear. The mid-wife says:

'Try not to push. The cord is round baby's neck. Don't worry, I'll cut it at the next contraction. Don't push even if you feel you want to.' After a few seconds I move forward again, the top of my head reaches the end of the tube and I feel something cold pressed against

14

my neck. Snip! I am released. My head pops out of the hole and the rest of me is pulled out with a twist. I am in a huge cold dry space. I open my mouth, take a big breath of air and a loud cry comes out. I am picked up, wrapped in a towel and put in Mummy's arms. My eyes are open and I can just see Mummy and Daddy. I stare at them and they gaze back at me.

The last day in Mummy's tummy is in fact the first day of the biggest adventure of all. I may not remember it when I am older, but today is the most important day of my life. Without it I would not be here.

A Pack of Lies

Muriel was delighted with her cabin on SS Magnolia. There was a balcony, an ensuite shower, plenty of storage space, and even a television. Not that she envisaged spending much time in her cabin, she was on a mission and all her time and energy would be devoted to that. She started to unpack her beautiful new clothes. Every now and then she stopped to hold an outfit up against herself in the mirror, imagining the admiring glances she would surely attract. Nobody would guess she was in her seventies with her neat figure, unblemished skin and golden hair. Would they?

She was there to find herself a man. He must be presentable, amusing, charming and, most important of all, rich. Where better to find one? Everyone knows widowers on the high seas are often on the lookout for a new partner. Muriel had spent years searching for a second husband but they had all managed to evade her. (Her husband had run off with a younger model many years earlier.) The clock was ticking. Over the years she had had several near misses. One had inconsiderately died the night before the wedding. Another had actually been married all along and had deceived her with a succession of lies for over four years. So Muriel had decided she would invest in a cruise, buy a whole wardrobe of flattering clothes, generally tart herself up and give it one more go. Being honest had done her no favours. Lying might do the trick. Judging by what she read online and in magazines, the truth was generally considered flexible nowadays anyway.

It was surprising how easy lying was. Muriel had recently joined a social club where she practised lying on a grand scale. She had invented a whole back story for herself, which included a glittering career as a model, a rich husband taken by a shark off Bondi Beach in Australia, and an apartment in New York. She was delighted at her level of proficiency, and how her new friends were taken in. She had treated her attendances there as a dry run, so to speak, for the cruise.

Some of her friends had experimented in online dating. But Muriel rightly ascertained that would attract even worse/better liars than her. So now here she was, putting her plan into action. She'd 'invested' a big lump of her savings to buy a place on the cruise. Let battle commence! She swanned down to dinner that first night made up to the nines and dressed exquisitely in scarlet silk. She was seated at a table with some experienced cruisers who managed tactfully to convey to her that what she was wearing would be ideal for the Captain's cocktail party the following evening. The next day she explored the decks, bars and lounges, seeking her prey.

After two days Muriel had ingratiated herself into a group of loud, friendly people, and spent most of her time with them, playing cards, drinking and taking advantage of the on board entertainment which included variety shows, films and ballroom dancing. There was one single man within the group. He was a widower, had plenty of hair, his own teeth, and seemed very taken with Muriel. His name was Rob. He admired her looks, he laughed at her jokes, he said he enjoyed her company. He accompanied Muriel on sightseeing trips ashore, and constantly sought her out on board. They started eating together every day at both lunch and dinner. Then they started meeting for breakfast too! They really hit it off with one another. Rob shared her sense of humour, he listened with interest and admiration to her fairy tales, and she reciprocated by encouraging him to talk about himself, obviously essential to their friendship, and hopefully, future relationship. It turned out he had plenty to say about himself. He was rich. He owned several houses and flats all over the world, he had no children, (whew!) he owned three racehorses and he was on the board of directors of several large companies.

Muriel could hardly believe her luck. It's one thing to make a life-changing plan but it's quite another to have it working out so spectacularly well. The cruise was in its last few days. She and Rob were making elaborate plans to meet up in London once they got back to the UK. He had strongly hinted at inviting her to stay in his mansion in Berkshire over Easter, which was only three weeks away.

He was still working part-time as a business consultant, and often had to go to New York on business. Muriel's (imaginary) apartment in New York rather worryingly came into the conversation, but she managed to remember she was allowing her god daughter to stay in it over the summer so would not be in New York at that time. It turned out Rob had a yacht, moored in the south of France. Did she like sailing? Muriel quickly realised that her fantasy life would certainly have included sailing. Oh yes, she loved it.

For the last night on board Muriel dressed for dinner with her usual care and attention. She wore again the blue taffeta gown she had worn the first time Rob had asked her to dance. Everything was fine. They sat together for what they called 'the last supper.' But of course it wasn't really. There would be plenty more suppers in the future. The next day they parted at the quayside with many hugs and mutual promises of texts and phone calls. Nothing concrete was arranged. No need with so many easy ways of making contact nowadays.

Hours later Muriel let herself into her cramped, shabby flat in an unfashionable part of London. She could hardly wait to start letting her friends know of her conquest. But something stopped her. She turned on her ipad and checked her phone for messages. Nothing from Rob. Of course he was a very busy man. She started unpacking and sorting out her immense pile of washing. Her imagination was leaping forward, as she began to work out how she would craftily tone down for Rob the actualities of her life; no apartment in New York, no amazing career, no… Her phone pinged. It was a text at last:

'Muriel, you silly old cow, did you really think I was taken in by all your stories? We are actually two of a kind. I'm not the business consultant, the company director, the yachtsman either. I was hoping to meet a rich widow to bail me out as I am in serious debt, but by the time I had realised you were a fraud it was too late as the cruise was nearly over. Be thankful you were not the person you made yourself out to be or I would have fleeced you dry. Rob by name, Rob by nature.'

Jack and the Beanstalk – A Tale of Our Time

'Jack, come 'ere.'

No reply. Then,

'Wot for?'

'Jack, come 'ere this minute or I'll give yer wot for!'

'Wot's up, Mum?'

I got this letter from the social. Me benefits been stopped it says 'ere.'

'Why's that then?'

His mum was clutching an official looking letter.
'I never went to the Job Centre when I should of. I missed the happointment. They're stopping me money. Jack, don't you go wandering off again. You take this letter and that dozy cow and get yourself down the food bank. I reckon you could exchange the cow for a couple of bags of groceries to keep us going till me benefits start up again. Make sure you get as much as you can. Off you go.'

Jack untied the rope round the neck of the family's last asset, Mabel, the cow. She'd been living in the garden as long as Jack could remember. She was nothing but a bag of bones and had long since stopped producing milk. Jack felt sad. He hoped he would not be the next to be evicted. The Bedroom Tax had hit his mother hard, she was now losing benefits each month because of the spare bedroom in their council house, and had threatened more than once to turn him out of the house so that she could go and live with her sister in Penge.

It was not far to the food bank, a landmark of poverty and need in the area. Jack tied Mabel's rope to the fence and went inside. When it came to his turn he produced the letter about the loss of his mother's benefits.

'I'm sorry, you can't just come here and collect food. And no, you can't exchange a cow for food either. I've heard it all now! There's another letter you need to have to show you qualify for help. I'm very sorry. I'll give you a form to take back to your mother.'

As he left Jack noticed a pile of tinned butter beans by the door. Quickly he picked up a tin and put it in his pocket. Then he looked around for Mabel, but she had gone. Her rope, still attached to the fence, lay on the ground but there was no cow at the other end.

Jack went home. When he told his mother what had happened she was incandescent with rage.

'You useless boy, I should never 'ave brought you 'ome from the 'ospital. You're nuffink but a waste of space. As for them beans, wot good are they to us?' So saying, she flung the tin out of the kitchen window into what might once have been a flower bed, where the tin landed on a vicious implement.

'Get aht there now and look for that cow.'

Poor Jack spent the rest of the day searching unsuccessfully for Mabel. She was well known on the estate but nobody had seen her. When night fell, hungry and exhausted, he curled up under a bush in a corner of the garden and fell asleep.

Jack awoke in the middle of the night to hear the rustling of leaves. He sat up and rubbed his eyes. Where the tin of beans had landed a huge plant had taken root, its massive leaves visible by the bright light of a full moon. Jack thought he must be dreaming. He started climbing up the beanstalk. After a few minutes, he emerged into bright sunlight. He found himself on a village green and heard a familiar sound. There was Mabel, happily grazing on some lush grass and gently mooing at the same time, to show her pleasure. Jack was delighted to see her. Then he looked around. A few yards away was a wall on which was sitting a large humanised egg. Before his very eyes the egg fell off the wall and broke into hundreds of pieces. A regiment of soldiers appeared and started trying to put the egg together again. Through an open door Jack saw an old woman looking in her cupboard for food. Her hungry dog was barking loudly. But the cupboard was bare. Three blind mice were scuttling away from a farmer's wife who was holding aloft their tails in one hand and brandishing a carving knife in the other. An amazing house in the shape of an enormous shoe caught his eye. It was full of children, all misbehaving and taking no notice of their harassed mother.

'Drink your broth without any bread,' she shouted at them. She picked up a cane, beat them all soundly and sent them to bed.

Jack decided to leave the scene of destruction and abuse. He returned to the beanstalk and started climbing once more, but as he reached the next level he spotted the shiny toe of a gigantic boot and heard a deep and terrifying voice roaring:

'Fee, fi, flick, flack, I smell the blood of a boy named Jack!'

So he clambered back down as fast as he could.

Mabel was still there. She followed him down the beanstalk. (Don't ask how.) Jack could still hear the giant uttering threats as they hastened towards safety. As soon as he and Mabel reached the garden Jack took an axe and chopped down the beanstalk. The giant and all the nursery rhyme characters were no more.

Jack's mother was overjoyed to see them, particularly as Mabel suddenly turned into a goose and started laying golden eggs. Jack, his mother and Mabel were able to leave social housing, and had no problem paying the exorbitant rents charged by greedy private landlords for the rest of their very happy lives.

Aatifa

My name is Aatifa and I come from Eritrea which is in East Africa. How my life has changed! Before and after school my brother Khalil and I used to help our mother, gathering firewood, fetching water from the river and looking after the animals. It was conscription that made my mother finally decide to leave. My father had been forced to join the army when I was very small. He was killed fighting in Ethiopia. Khalil was getting near the age when he would have to do national service. There is no limit to how long he would be in the army and our mother did not want my brother to go. On top of that my country has one of the worst human rights records in the whole world, similar to North Korea. I want to be a journalist when I'm older and in Eritrea there is no freedom of the press, all information is provided by the government and many journalists have been thrown into prison. So there were good reasons for both me and my brother to leave Eritrea and of course our mother did not want us to go alone. So we sold everything we had and borrowed money from relatives as well to pay the people smugglers who promised to take us to the UK.

In Europe we hoped to have a better life but we knew it would be a long and difficult journey. We did not realise when we set off one night carrying some food and a few clothes just what was in store for us and all the other people we met along the way. We saw so many people die on the journey. We walked for weeks, through the forests of Ethiopia. Every night we heard hyenas howling, it was very scary. Eventually we reached the Sudan.

The people in Sudan did not like us because we are Christians. We stayed in a very small house for several weeks with dozens of others, and we were not even allowed to go outside. Eventually we got places on a lorry going to Libya. More people died in the lorry and were left by the roadside. In Libya we lived in a filthy camp where my mother became ill and weak. There was little food or medical help. Even water was rationed. After four months we were told we would be going on a boat to Europe.

It was not a real boat, just a rubber dinghy. It sat very low in the water because there were so many people on board. The man who arranged for us to go took the last of our money. We were crammed in tightly and could not lie down to sleep. Despite everything I was excited when we started off but the next day the sea was quite rough and the boat began taking in water. We tried our best to bale it out, but too many people moved to one side and it started to capsize. There were no lifejackets. Most of us were tipped into the sea. My brother could swim and so could I but not my mother. She was not strong. She clung to the side of the boat, but she quickly grew cold and exhausted. Her eyes were starting to close, and then we saw a bigger boat coming to rescue us. I begged her to be brave and keep hanging on but she let go and slipped under the water. My brother dived down to bring her back and between us we kept her afloat until the rescuers arrived. They did check to see if she was alive, but when they saw that she had drowned they let her slip back into the sea again. She was not the only one, another woman, an old man, three babies and two small children were also left in the sea.

Khalil and I were numb with grief. There are no words to say how we felt. We had been through terrible dangers to get this far and now we would have to continue the journey on our own. We had never felt so alone, even though we were surrounded by hundreds of people. We had not eaten for days. On board the rescue ship we were given food and there was space to lie down. After two days we saw land ahead. It was Italy. We were not allowed to go ashore. The Italians did not want any more refugees. People on board were very worried and scared. We thought we would have to go back to Libya. One man was so desperate he threatened to jump into the sea. Malta also refused to accept us. The boat set off again and reached Spain who took pity on us and we went ashore. There was much singing and great relief.

Now Khalil and I are living in a refugee camp in Spain, and we are looking after a little girl, Fatimah, whose parents both died in Libya. She was put on our boat and has no-one to look out for her.

Khalil and I have told the officials that we want to go to England. That is where our mother wanted us to go. She had heard that it is a very great country with lots of people from all over the world living happily together. I think it is very hard to get to England as people have told us they do not like refugees there now either. I am glad my mother never found out that she was wrong about England. I still hope to become a journalist and Khalil wants to study engineering. We pray every night that we shall be able to go somewhere in Europe where we can live safely, without fear, rebuild our lives and have the future our mother planned for us.

Samson and Delilah

You remember the advertisement for Diet Coke that showed women lusting after a hunky man? It was like that with Samson. All the girls fancied him. He worked on a building site next door to the further education college. As the female students stepped off the bus each morning they would search for a glimpse of his amazing torso. His bare top was a popular local attraction with the ladies. Rows of muscles shimmered under his olive skin as he lifted hods of bricks ten times as large as anyone else could manage, dragged trailers of hard core single handedly or moved the occasional skip, empty or full. His long locks of wavy black hair added to his striking appearance.

Samson was rumoured to be an illegal immigrant, from somewhere in the middle east. He knew little English but he was greatly respected for his amazing strength. He was a valuable asset to the workforce, doing the work of at least twenty men every day.

The owner of the building company soon became aware that his site manager had hired an outstanding worker, and he came down to see Samson for himself. Stanley Fastbuck could barely believe what he saw. Samson had a concrete mixer tucked under one arm while he pulled a trolley holding five tons of paving stones with the other. Pound signs flashed before Stanley's eyes. He made enquiries from his office staff and sensibly decided to start paying Samson a decent bonus amounting to almost double his usual pay, for doing the work of twenty men every day. By a combination of mime and the exchange of broken English this news was conveyed to Samson, who seemed pleased, and smiled his devastating smile.

It was too much to expect that news of the amazing Samson would not spread, and spread it did. Before long there were many builders, ranging from fully qualified members of the Chartered Institute of Building to fully unqualified members of the cowboy fraternity, beating a path to Samson's door and offering him a great deal of money, free accommodation and even British citizenship if he would come and work for them. But Samson would not be bought. He was happy working next door to the college, he already had lodgings, and he was loyal to site manager, Charlie. As for the extra money he was being offered, he said to himself, in his own language, the equivalent of 'There's no such thing as a free lunch.'

However the day came when he was offered something he could not resist, an auburn- headed beauty, Delilah, the daughter of Stanley Fastbuck's greatest rival, Sidney Bombdamage. Delilah arrived on the number 43 bus. As usual, there was a group of young women ogling the half-dressed paragon of desirability, Samson. It was raining and the water dropping off his raven locks added to his attraction as he shinned up and down ladders carrying multiple hods of tiles. Delilah shoved her way to the front of the group, opened her scarlet lips and called in husky tones:

'Samson!' Fate stepped in and Samson responded. To cut a long story short, they soon became an item, (as it doesn't say in the Bible).

It was not long before Delilah asked Samson the $64,000 dollar question:

'How come you're so strong?'

Samson prevaricated, but in the end he told her that it was due to the fact that he always slept at the wrong end of the bed, which indeed he did.

'Why don't you try sleeping at the right end, with me tonight?' suggested Delilah, sweetly.

So he did and next day his strength was not affected.

'Samson, you told me a porky,' Delilah challenged. 'Please tell me the real secret of your power.'

'OK', replied Samson, his English having evolved by leaps and bounds due to his association with Delilah.

'I am so strong because I always open boiled eggs at the pointy end.' Another porky.

'I am so strong because I step on the cracks between paving stones.'

And so it went on. 'I am so strong because…'

26

'Enough!' screeched Delilah. She had been getting a combination of hassle and bribes from her dad, Sidney Bombdamage.

'OK, it's in my hair. I have never cut my hair in my whole life. If my hair is cut my strength, it will be gone.'

That night as he lay sleeping, Delilah cut off Samson's beautiful black locks.

Samson's career was over.

When he went to work next day nobody recognised him.

'Me Samson, me Samson,' his standard of English having deteriorated due to shock, he repeated desperately to Charlie. But his strength had gone and so had his value on the building site. Charlie called the authorities and Samson was arrested as an illegal immigrant. He was eventually deported after spending months incarcerated in a detention centre. He never saw Delilah again. Sidney Bombdamage had destroyed Stanley Fastbuck's trump card.

Nine months later Delilah gave birth to a baby boy with long, thick locks of black hair.

Glass Half Full

Meriel was waiting for a telephone call from her grown up daughter. She had learned over the years since Lesley left home that the way to control the dread, always part of awaiting such calls, was to keep herself as busy as possible. She had therefore embarked on a full scale spring clean of the living room, to include washing the net curtains, polishing the windows and dusting the books individually.

Brian passed by the open door on his way out to play golf. He was not a new man. He had long since decided that his role was to bring home the bacon and little else. He was not prepared to cope with the emotional realities of modern life as experienced by his grown up daughter. He left all that to Meriel.

'I see Lesley has decided to ruin our weekend,' he remarked nastily, and he was gone. A familiar twinge of distress briefly overwhelmed Meriel. There had been a time when she would have remonstrated with him for making such a hateful remark about Lesley. But now she accepted it as part and parcel of her marriage. After all, Brian was a good man, deep down. 'Very deep,' her best friend Barbara would, and in fact did, often say. Just because he was not, as far as she knew, a bigamist, or a murderer, did that make him OK?

Occasionally Meriel played with the idea of divorcing Brian. It was a special 'get out of jail free' card she allowed herself to daydream about when he had been particularly unkind. His speciality was belittling her both in private and in public, as well as limiting communication to remarks designed to hurt her. As she dusted, polished and hoovered she tried to guess what Lesley would have in store to upset her about today. Last week it had been a falling-out with her flatmates, threatening the security of her accommodation. Other frequent themes were crises with boy friends, 'misunderstandings' at work and, unsurprisingly, loneliness.

Lesley was in fact a qualified accountant with a good job, but her personality, obviously inherited from her father, made her dealings with others problematic. It had always been the same. Her reports bore witness to this all through her schooldays. Comments such as 'Lesley is an excellent student, but unfortunately her inability to get on with her class mates makes difficulties for her and upsets other students.' were a hint of future problems. In fact the school had suggested that their daughter needed help to cope with her problems, but of course Brian had poo-poohed such an idea.

'Lesley just needs to learn to be reasonable and get on with people' he had declared, failing to recognise advice he himself needed to follow.

As a break from her self-inflicted domestic chores, Meriel sat down and picked up a magazine she had found among the books. Naturally she was drawn to the problem pages, always the most interesting and readable section. Who can resist reading about those with more intractable problems than one's own? Among the usual sad accounts of domestic and emotional trauma she came upon a letter that might actually have been written by her.

'*Dear Catherine, I am at my wits end. My husband of forty years is a selfish git. He offers no support to our grown-up son who seems unable to cope with normal life. He lacks the ability to empathise with others in any way whatsoever. I am sick and tired of making suggestions about counselling and other ways in which he might be helped, all of which my husband says are not necessary, therefore not supporting either me or our son. I have tried to persuade him to seek medical help, to no avail. He is on the brink of losing his job because of his problems in dealing with people. On top of that he has taken up gambling and is on the slippery slope to bankruptcy. What shall I do?*' Catherine's reply was decisive.

'*I sympathise with the very difficult situation you are in. There are two strands to your troubles, your husband and your son. Because you have been married for forty years does not mean that you cannot end your marriage. I know divorce is a huge step but please do consider it. Obviously your son is causing you a lot of heartache, and from your longer letter, and after consulting a psychiatrist I suggest your son needs to go to his GP and seek help for his mental health. It may well be that, as you have already realised, counselling would be of benefit to him, but he needs to make these decisions himself. You cannot force your son to take any action. So try to stop banging your head against a brick wall, you have done all you can. Learn to step back, look after yourself and think seriously about your marriage.'*

Meriel read and re-read the letter. Then she made a resolution. She would follow Catherine's advice. Just because neither her husband nor her daughter were capable of change, it did not mean that she must play the victim card. It would not be easy, but nor was life at present. The telephone rang.

'Hello Lesley, how are things?' She listened to her daughter's rants.

'Lesley, I have heard all this before. I know you have a lot of problems coping with people. Please take my advice and go and try to get some help. If you need me to pay for counselling... Lesley, please don't interrupt. I'm going now as I'm busy. Do let me know what you decide. I cannot help you if you won't help yourself. I love you,' and she put the phone down. Never before had she been so abrupt with Lesley, but it was time to try a different approach. The next job was to find out all about divorce. She would begin by asking Barbara. She'd had plenty of experience in that area.

Meriel felt invigorated. There was a spring in her step. She rang Barbara and asked if she could come round for a cup of tea. She put on her coat. She would be out when Brian came home. There would be no dinner waiting for him. He always found something unkind to say about her cooking. Let him cook his own. If she stuck to her guns, from being half empty, her glass should soon be half full.

How it Was

Becky looked hard at herself in the triple mirror on her dressing table. It was very small, only her head and shoulders showed. Her dark hair was hanging straight down as usual, her face was a little flushed but nothing had actually changed. That was a relief. She pressed her hands down her body to her waist. Was it her imagination or was her waist thickening a little? Her hands moved to her stomach. Was that a hint of a bump? For the umpteenth time she consulted the flowery calendar on her bedroom wall, a present last Christmas, 1962, from Auntie Ethel. It was not a bad dream. She was now three weeks late.

'Are you seeing that boy again this evening, Becky?' Her mum asked, as she bent down to take the cottage pie out of the oven.

'His name's Clark.'

'That's a job, not a name,' her mother retorted, 'and watch your tongue, young lady. You're too young to be running round with boys anyway. Just because you've left school doesn't mean you can do what you like. You've got a good job with the council, you need to work hard and show them what you can do. There'll be plenty of time for boyfriends when you're a bit older, like our Sally.'

Sally, Becky's older sister, was engaged to a very proper and boring young man she'd met at her office Christmas party two years earlier. Becky told her friends you could fall asleep just by looking at him. Sally seemed happy, saving up for the wedding, buying items for her bottom drawer and looking forward to an all too predictable future. Their lives were all mapped out before them. Becky was different, she dreamed of living in London, and being discovered by a talent scout. She was pretty, she could sing, she could dance.

Just for a few seconds Becky had forgotten about the late period. The idea of being an unmarried mother made her feel sick. There had been a girl in Sally's class who had 'got into trouble.' She was lucky, her parents supported her and she was allowed to stay at home and keep the baby. He was now a toddler. Becky saw him sometimes with his mum and grandmother. Nobody spoke to that family. Becky knew her parents would not be so understanding. To them unmarried mothers were immoral and evil. And as for marrying Clark, even she realised that would not work. Clark was definitely not husband material. He had quite a reputation among the local girls which is no doubt why Becky had fallen for his charms.

When Clark arrived on his motor bike that evening Becky determined to tell him she though she might be pregnant. It was hard to believe that the hasty, and if truth be told, painful coupling that had taken place behind the bus shelter several times in the past few weeks, might have resulted in a baby. There, she had said the dreaded word to herself. Baby. Becky actually loved babies, not that she'd ever had much to do with them. For a minute she allowed herself the fantasy of holding her own new baby, feeding him, pushing him out in a pram.

It proved harder than she thought to break the news of impending fatherhood to Clark, but his reaction was swift and surprisingly business-like.

'How late are yer? Have yer thrown up yet? Does yer mum know?' It was a relief to share the news with someone else, but at the same time it made it seem more real.

'I'll tell yer what Becky. Wait a few more days 'cos you might just be late. But if not I know someone who can get rid of it for yer. It's against the law but this ex-nurse, she'll do it for £100. I know it's a lot of money but she's risking going to prison if she gets found out. Can yer get your hands on that sort of money?' Becky's head was spinning. This woman would kill her baby. But the terrible worry hanging over her would be gone. And where could she find £100? She did have some money in national savings certificates but her mother kept the book. It crossed Becky's mind that Clark seemed remarkably well prepared for the scenario he'd described. Perhaps her mum was right about Clark after all. His small pointy face which she had thought endearing suddenly took on the appearance of a rat.

Becky's mum was pleased that her daughter no longer seemed to be interested in that Clark, and Becky felt emboldened to ask her mother if she could have her savings book to pay for a typing and shorthand course in the evenings. Meanwhile time was passing and Becky had been sick twice early in the morning. She blamed it on food she'd eaten in the canteen at work.

Becky made the arrangements secretly with Clark, telling her mum she was visiting her friend. During days at the office she managed to avoid thinking about what she was about to do and just concentrated on her work. She stopped looking at babies in their prams. Even her mum noticed she was not herself and bought her some cod liver oil and malt to buck her up. That really did make Becky sick. In bed at night she wept. She went over her options time after time. but there seemed to be no other way out.

The day came. Becky had booked a half-day off work.

'Doing something nice?' asked one of her colleagues. Becky caught the train to where the alleged ex-nurse lived. She found the road, a down-at-heel row of small terraced houses. The address she was looking for had filthy bedraggled net curtains in the window. Becky knocked on the door. She had no choice.

Medusa's Revenge

The shrill sound of the bell indicated the start of the school day at St.Saviour's School. Miss Cobra, Deputy Head, was on duty, checking uniforms and ensuring that no trainers were masquerading as school shoes.

'Johnnie, where's your tie?'

'Dunno, Miss'.

'Report to me at break. If it hasn't turned up by then you will be doing a detention after school.'

'Grace, remove all that make-up. This is a school, not a film studio.'

Miss Cobra was not known for mincing her words. However, her quest to spot evidence of Johnnie's, Grace's and several other pupils' uniform malfunction and make-up application that morning caused her not to spot a pupil wearing a hoodie slip behind her and make her way along the corridor to her classroom.

Members of Class 5B were waiting for registration, in their usual undisciplined manner. If anything the noise level increased when their form teacher, Mr Adder, hurried into the room, clutching several folders and looking harassed. A newly qualified teacher, he was beginning to regret his choice of career. In his anxiety to take the register quickly Mr Adder ignored the fact several members of his class were still wearing their coats, strictly not allowed. One of them was even wearing a hoodie.

'Five B, Five B please be quiet. I need to take the register. No, Ali. you may not go to the toilet. You've only been in school five minutes. Now, please settle down all of you.'

Meanwhile in the school office the telephone was ringing constantly. Some of the calls were from parents explaining that their son or daughter was unwell and would not be coming to school. A couple were from students pretending to be their own parents, also explaining that their daughter or son was unwell and would not be coming to school. Mrs Viper, the secretary, had devised a cunning plan to catch the phoney phone-callers, and was busy ringing the place of work of one of the alleged parents, to check the story.

Class Five B, registration having at last been accomplished, made its straggly way to the first lesson of the day, science. Miss Cobra went to her office to draw up a long list of uniform deniers she would see at break. They would need to come up with an impressive reason for not being suitably attired, to escape an hour's after school detention, or even a two hour detention in the case of serial offenders. St.Saviour's School prided itself on its strict discipline policy and its insistence on adherence to the school's rules and regulations. The school's 'Outstanding' Ofsted rating had recently been downgraded to 'Good' and the slippery slope towards 'Requires Improvement' beckoned. Of course the quality of teaching was of prime importance, and newly qualified teachers such as Mr Adder, who were failing to live up to the promise they had displayed at interview, was another problem pending for the school's senior management team.

In the school office the telephone calls were becoming less frequent. The next call was from the local paper. Mrs Viper braced herself for bad news. In her experience calls from that quarter were usually based on reports featuring the misdemeanours of St.Saviour's pupils. This one was different.

'I wonder if you can confirm that a pupil at your school was married over the weekend?'

Mrs Viper was not the head's right hand woman for nothing.

'No comment' she replied swiftly.

'It's strange that she should get married on Saturday and be back in school on Monday.'

'It would be if it was true, replied the secretary.

'Don't you want to know who it is?'

'I'm sure you're going to tell me'.

'The girl's name is Medusa Gorgon and she married a bloke called Poseidon.'

Mss Viper hung up. Medusa Gorgon was a strange girl. She had once made the mistake of swearing at Miss Cobra in Greek, not

35

knowing that the Deputy Head could speak Greek too. The Deputy head had taken her revenge on Medusa with a whole host of sanctions and punishments. There was no love lost between them.

Far away, the goddess Athena had heard the news. Her beautiful hand maiden Medusa, the only mortal Gorgon, had broken her vow of chastity. Athena had acted swiftly.

In the science lab Medusa Gorgon was at last being told to remove her hoodie. As she took it off the pupils nearest to her starting screaming. In a few seconds the whole class erupted in chaos, and Mr Anaconda, the science teacher, had run for his life, The students could not believe their eyes. In place of her beautiful black hair Medusa's head was alive with snakes, hissing and flashing their forked tongues. Some of them dropped to the ground, writhing in every direction as the whole class rushed out of the lab. Medusa, the child bride, shook her head, but as snakes fell to the ground more and more appeared, frantically swaying in the air..

News of what had happened spread like wildfire throughout the school and most teachers told their classes to leave school immediately and go home, and did the same themselves. However Miss Cobra was made of sterner stuff. With Ofsted still uppermost in her mind, she stayed in school, standing in the doorway nearest to the labs. Medusa left the lab and made for the main building, her hair writhing freely. She stared at Miss Cobra, who stared back. The Deputy Head turned to stone.

The Ghost of Owl Cottage

It was a still summer day, no breeze rustled the leaves in the wood surrounding the derelict cottage. A young couple drew up in front of the property. A warped 'For Sale' sign indicated they had reached their destination. A cat, snoozing in the bushes, awoke and slunk off into the wood.

Elspeth and Peter stepped out of their car and stood in front of Owl Cottage.

'It needs a lot doing to it. The roof's in a bad way and I would be surprised if there's not considerable water damage inside,' pronounced Peter.

'Unlock the door, Peter. I can't wait to see inside. I've always wanted to live somewhere really old,' was Elspeth's rejoinder.

It was dark inside the cottage where peeling wallpaper and huge cobwebs hanging from every corner demonstrated its abandoned state. Of course the electricity was turned off but their eyes soon adjusted to the darkness and they liked what they saw. There were a lot of repairs to be done but, surprisingly, not a lot of damage due to rain.

'I'm rather surprised the asking price is so low,' remarked Peter as they made their way back to their car. 'OK it needs money spent on it but there are four bedrooms and loads of scope for improvement. I guess we're just lucky Dad's a builder.'

'I love the back garden. It's totally surrounded by trees. Did you see that old swing tied to one of the overhanging branches? It was swaying to and fro as if someone had just jumped off it.'

'Are you sure about that, Ellie? There's absolutely no wind today.'

"Yes, I thought it was quite strange.'

'I'm going back to check that swing,' Peter was followed by Elspeth. This time they squeezed round the side of the cottage, where a narrow, overgrown path led to the back garden. There was the swing, attached to an overhanging branch. But it hung still.

'Well, it was moving before. I'm sure it was,' Elspeth insisted.

Elspeth and Peter bought Owl Cottage. They were new to the area and were unaware of the belief among the locals that it was haunted. Anyway they were modern young people and probably would not have taken much notice of hearsay. This was a bargain and not only did they love it, they also stood to make a hefty profit in a few years time when it had been renovated and they would sell it, buy another run-down property and restore that.

Owl Cottage was duly repaired, renovated and transformed into a charming, desirable property. In due course Elspeth became pregnant. Everything was going to plan for the couple. The baby duly arrived, a daughter they named Harriet, her parents pride and joy. She was a happy child with dark, sparkling eyes, light brown curls and a beautiful smile.

When Harriet was about eighteen months old Elspeth found a stray cat in the garden. She was completely black with piercing bright yellow eyes. Elspeth and Peter both liked cats so they adopted her and named her Amber. Unknown to them, Amber had been there the day they first viewed Owl Cottage. Amber was devoted to Harriet and allowed the toddler to play with her and even pick her up. She never lifted a paw against Harriet although she sometimes hissed at Peter and Elspeth.

At about the same time as Amber joined the family, Elspeth occasionally became aware of a presence passing through the cottage. She also noticed that Harriet looked up and stopped whatever she was doing at the same time. Peter was very down to earth about these visitations.

'Ellie, it's the cat wandering about, it must be. Some of the floorboards upstairs are quite creaky. That's what Harriet is hearing. Stands to reason.' Of course it never happened when Peter was home, and Elspeth could not be sure if Amber was in the house at the time anyway.

The months and years flew by. The plan to sell Owl Cottage was underway. Harriet would soon be starting school and the couple were buying another old property not far from the school. She was four and a half years old. It was the day before they moved out. Her parents were in the kitchen, packing up their pots and pans. Harriet was in the back garden, playing on the swing.while Amber lay fully stretched out on the grass, soaking up the last afternoon sunshine.

'Harriet, come inside now, it's time for your bath,' called Elspeth from the back door. She glanced over at the swing. It was moving back and forth. Harriet and Amber had vanished.

The police were on the scene within a few minutes. Tracker dogs were called in. The wood behind Owl Cottage was searched. Road blocks were set up. The search was widened. Appeals were made on national television. It was all in vain. Harriet was never found.

Amber returned to Owl Cottage nine months later. The new family had a little boy, he was just eighteen months old.

The Best of Intentions

My Bert passed away four weeks ago today. It was such a shock. One minute there he was, large as life and twice as natural, as my old Gran used to say. Then it happened. We'd had a busy old morning. Bert had been out in the garden, tidying up the leaves that always land in our garden even though we have no trees, and I had decided to tackle the spare room which hadn't seen the Hoover since before Christmas. He turned down the digestive biscuit he always had with his coffee, which was a bad sign in itself, thinking back. Anyway he'd just lifted his cup, but he put it down again without drinking. His face went red and then he slumped forward onto the table, sending the coffee flying. I tried to remember my first aid training from years ago, but all I could think of was 999.

Bert had had a stroke and never regained consciousness. He'd always been so healthy, he'd never even taken blood pressure tablets. I'm glad really that he didn't come round. He wouldn't have been the same after a stroke. He would have hated to be disabled in any way, and he was a good age, eighty-nine. But I miss him terribly. I know it sounds ridiculous but I'd never stopped and imagined what life would be like without him. We had three children, and we both worked, so there was never much time for thinking about the future. Once we retired we still kept busy, and the time passed by so quickly we wondered how we'd ever found time to go to work.

Four weeks later

My Denise has been such a help with all the paperwork and arrangements. Bert's funeral was dreadful. Even now I can't put into words what it was like. People said he had 'a good send-off' as if he was there enjoying it all. I had to bite my tongue I can tell you. Anyway, Denise has started making suggestions about what she calls 'finding a home' for Bert's clothes, and his fishing gear and of course the car, since I don't drive. But I'm not ready to part with any of these things.

She asked me today why I haven't cancelled the local paper that Bert used to read every week, but again I told her I'm not ready.

'But Mum,' she argued, 'you're paying for something you never read.'

'I don't care,' I said, 'I just like to hear it popping through the letter-box like it always has.'

She changed the subject then.

'I could take Dad's clothes to the charity shop, when you're ready, ' she added. She's been staying with me since Bert died.

'It will be a while until I can come and stay again so it's a good chance to get Dad's clothes out of the house and to people who need them.'

'Thanks Denise, I'll let you know.' I didn't tell her I'll never be ready. I didn't tell her I can't seem even to throw away anything Bert used or liked, or that we'd bought when he was here. I've a strange compulsion to keep everything connected with him. Even the wrappings from food he liked, empty tins, bottles, everything goes into boxes and bags. It's the only way I can face life without him. I can't explain it because it is ridiculous, but that's just how I am. I'm trying to hide it from Denise because I don't want to hear what she has to say.

Six months later

Most of my friends have stopped coming round. When they do come they either pretend to ignore the bags and boxes of stuff I have filled up or they offer to get rid of them for me. I suspect gossip has been taking place. So I've decided to stop letting them in any more. It's none of their business. My neighbour Mary even had the cheek to say it was dangerous that I have boxes on the stairs.

'None of your business,' I muttered what I thought was under my breath, but I think she heard because she got up and left.

'Let me know when you want to go to the tip, before it finishes coming to you,' she offered as her parting shot.

Eight months later

I can't open the front door any more. There's such a lot of things I need to hold on to. It makes me feel safe, as if Bert is still here. I know it sounds silly. I've started storing bags in the car now. Who cares what the neighbours think? I've got a bit of a problem though. Denise is coming to stay. Her old bedroom is jam-packed. I'm getting in such a state worrying about it. Before she left after Bert died she made me promise to start having a bit of a turn-out. She said it would make me feel better. When she rings, which she does every weekend, I make up a little story of what I've been doing, like spring cleaning for example. I'm going to have to ask her not to come.

Just had a visit from Mary next door. Apparently Denise rang her to ask if I was alright as she thought it strange I had asked her not to come. Mary told her about my bags of stuff and offered to get someone to come and take it all away. Denise said to go ahead. Bloody cheek. So a man with a van is coming in the morning...I don't know what to do...I can't cope...I must keep everything that reminds me of Bert...

Ten Days Later

Headline in local paper

WIDOW TAKES OWN LIFE

If Only...

In November 2018 the Culture Secretary said: 'Lego helps me switch off from stress.'

The play leader and her two assistants arrived at the back door of No.10 Downing Street. They were greeted by the Cabinet Secretary and ushered into an ante-room where the Official Secrets Act was read out to them. It was made very clear that contravening the terms of the act was tantamount to treason and would result in a long custodial sentence. It was also explained that if any one of them, individually, broke the vow of silence to which they were about to commit themselves, by speaking, writing, tweeting, emailing, texting, messaging, telephoning or communicating in any way whatsoever with any living person, known or unknown, related or not, and in any language, they would all be liable to the aforementioned long custodial sentence.

Karen had only recently met her colleagues, at a special reception, part of the interviewing process. The aim was to ascertain how they behaved in a social setting, and how they dealt with normal conversational enquiries about their work. They has been recruited by an agency experienced in finding people to fill important and sensitive roles in government, roles which it was considered essential to classify as 'top secret'. Such roles were not subject to enquiries made via the Freedom of Information Act. The whole process of recruiting the women had taken several months. Their backgrounds had been investigated, their private lives monitored and their characters thoroughly scrutinised. It had all been carried out in such a clandestine manner that they had not even been totally aware of what had taken place.

Karen felt a terrible urge to laugh. She managed to control it. Pamela, the most experienced of them, was looking shell-shocked as was Frances whose pale face matched her ash blond hair. Perhaps the Cabinet Secretary sensed that it was time to move on. Briskly he concluded the warnings and asked them to sign the document. He shook them all by the hand, wished them luck and handed them over to another official called Jack.

Jack was refreshingly normal.

'Now all that palaver is out of the way I'll take you to the playroom. It can be reached directly from the cabinet office so there's no risk that members of staff here at No.10 will see the toys. Mum's the word!' he added with a grin. He led them down a narrow corridor to a room marked 'Supplies'.

'i shall unlock this room for you each week before the cabinet meeting is over. I'll come and find you in here,' indicating a small waiting room nearby. 'You'll soon get used to the routine. Today I have arranged the room for you but usually you will get here in time to get out the equipment and prepare for the session.'

He unlocked the door. What a sight met their eyes. It was exactly like a very well-equipped playgroup, but with bigger chairs and tables. There was Play-Doh, Lego, a house corner with dolls, a cot and a toy oven, an easel with paints, drawing paper, felt tips, crayons, pictures to cut out with real scissors and glue, jigsaw puzzles, and best of all – a great big dressing up box full of pirate costumes, stylish evening dresses, soldiers' and nurses' uniforms and several scary face masks. There was a buggy with a doll in it, a scooter and a keyboard.

'How did you know what to buy?' asked Karen.

'That was easy,' Jack replied,' we sent round a memo containing a questionnaire to all cabinet members, asking them which toys they thought would help them relax after the weekly meeting. They all replied immediately, which is not what normally happens.'

'They must have cost a lot of money. We have to hold jumble sales and coffee mornings if we want to buy toys for our playgroups,' said Pamela.

'Yes, they did,' Jack admitted, 'but there's always funding available for important government projects.'

Just then a different door opened and the members of the cabinet filed into the room. When they saw the lay-out of toys Karen, Pamela and Frances were almost knocked down by the rush. They watched in amazement as the adults swooped on the toys with shrieks of delight. In no time they were busily occupied. The men flung off their jackets and crouched on the floor with bricks, cars and skittles, joined by the women who quickly removed their uncomfortable shoes. All were soon involved in engrossing play. There was a bit of a tussle in one corner where the bulging dressing up box was situated. It involved the Home Secretary, the Minister for Culture and a dashing red velvet gown trimmed with sequins. Pamela resolved the dispute, persuading the two of them to wear it in turns. Obviously the Lego was a big attraction. Several of the participants admitted to playing with it at home after their children had gone to bed. One minister admitted to relief at not feeling guilty at spending time on Lego:

'But this is different, it's part of our working day.'

After an hour and a half, they were told to move their chairs into a big circle and were given a glass of orange squash and two plain biscuits. To finish they all enjoyed a gusty sing-song of nursery rhymes and children's songs, led by Frances on the keyboard. The Chancellor of the Exchequer raised his hand and asked Karen if they could have story time next week? His special favourite was 'The Magic Porridge Pot.' The session ended with Karen reminding them that these toy therapy sessions were a very special and important secret and she trusted them not to break the promise to keep it they had already made to the Prime Minister. Jack came back and the adults departed, leaving Karen and her colleagues to put away all the toys in a large enclosed storage area at the far end of the room. Jack checked that the room had been returned to the status quo, locked the door and escorted the three ladies to the back door of No.10.

Over the following months something unique in political history took place. First the media and then even the public began to notice a sea change in the Westminster village. There emerged an improved spirit of co-operation among cabinet members, and it spread not only to back benchers but to members of other parties too. The cabinet set an example of good behaviour, not only in the House of Commons but also in the real world. As a result, for the first time ever, the government of the day became increasingly popular, and British politics entered a new golden age. Political parties agreed to take turns at being in power, ending the need for general elections and thereby saving all concerned both time and money. And nobody let the cat out of the bag about what took place behind the door marked 'Supplies'!

Back Inside

Most of the cons on the wing thought I was off me 'ead. Bert, who's been inside nearly as long as me, even suggested I ask to see the quack. Bert's got another five years before he can even apply for parole. He 'accidentally' shot someone when he was on a job at a big house in the country. They thought the house was unoccupied.

'Why d'ya take a gun if there wasn't supposed to be no-one there?' I asked him when he first arrived.

'Well, there was someone there, that's why I shot 'im.' Sometimes it's hard to get a straight answer out of Bert. His defence lawyer had the same trouble, which might be why he ended up with such a long sentence.

Anyway, to get back to what I said to make them think I was crackers. Inside's like 'ome to me. I was taken into care when I was a little kid, just three years old. Or so I've been told. Can't really remember it meself. I never had no dad, and my mum had seven of us. She was on the game and when she got put inside, that's when we was sent to the children's 'ome. At first me sister and two of me brothers was in there with me. But later we was all split up. I remember just one time when me mum come to see me when I was about seven, but she couldn't take me 'ome, and after that I never saw her no more. As I got older I was sent to other 'omes, and even fostered out a couple of times, but nobody ever wanted to keep me, I was that much trouble. I had a habit of stealing cars and joy riding around. Of course I kept getting caught and in no time I found meself in borstal, as it was then.

After borstal me career really took off. I'd learned so much from the other lads, and I joined a gang what done big robberies all over the country. We was all specialists. I started off as the driver because of my experience in pinching cars, but later I learned how to pick locks and then started working on safes. I was put away more times than I can remember, and at first I couldn't wait to get out. Having no place to go I always ended up in 'ostels for the 'omeless.

But I had a stroke of luck. Not on the 'orses, but sumthink even better. I got a probation officer who really tried to help me go straight. Him and my social worker managed to fix things so that I had me own flat. It was great, me first real 'ome. I'd only been in the flat about five weeks when there was a knock on the door one night. I knew it weren't the police. It was too quiet, and for once I had a clear conscience. It was Jimmy, one of the old gang.

'How's tricks, Steve?'

'Come in Jimmy, good to see you. Want a cuppa tea? I ain't got nuffink stronger.'

'Nice little gaff you got 'ere,' said Jimmy as he stepped inside. We sat down for a fag and a chat. It turned out Jimmy had been out of prison for several months and truly believed the Old Bill had forgotten all about 'im. 'e'd been going straight too and was hopeful that 'is old woman was about to take him back.

'The thing is Steve, I really need a few bob to get back in my Tracey's good books. I was 'oping you'd do just one more job with me. The kids need their dad.'

'Sorry, Jimmy, I ain't doing no more robbing. If I go back inside I'll lose this place.'

But in the end he wore me down. It was just going to be the one job. Jewellery again, our speciality. We knew where we could flog it, the safe was an easy one. What could possibly go wrong?

Don't ask. Everythink. The Old Bill did remember Jimmy and it didn't take them long to find 'im. 'e'd just moved back with 'is family. Of course they put two and two together and recognised my handiwork too. We both ended up inside again.

I wasn't getting any younger and I started worrying about my future. That's when I told my mates about my plan to get back inside for a nice long sentence. Eventually another chance for parole came up and I got it on the second attempt. I'd had plenty of experience of how to work the system and I 'adn't caused no trouble. As the date for my release grew closer I realised I was right. I wasn't looking forward to getting out. Obviously I'd never get another chance of a flat. I was getting too old for them 'ostels. Inside it was warm, I'd plenty of mates, three meals a day, why would I want to be outside? 'arassment from the cops every time something somewhere goes missing, nowhere to live except a cardboard box in a doorway.

Release day. They give us a few bob. I made for the shops. The toy shop said they didn't stock guns no more. I quite understood, but said I'd promised me grandson one for 'is birthday. Sometimes I surprise meself with what I come up with. Then I went in a newsagent's to get some fags. There on a stand were realistic toy guns in see-through packaging. I bought one. I unwrapped the gun and put the wrapping in a bin. Didn't want to be 'ad up for dropping litter, nowhere near bad enough! Next stop the bank. Out came the gun and the words I'd practised saying back in me cell…

Now I'm safely back inside. Job done.

The Brief Life of a Bunch of Flowers

I consisted of four dark red gerberers, three stalks of dark green foliage, five purple stocks and several white carnations.

In the evening, after the market stall was closed and we were covered over with tarpaulin in readiness for the next day, we bunches of flowers discussed where we were likely to end up. The pretty pink ones, tied up with curled ribbon and wrapped in decorative cellophane, imagined themselves destined for a romantic gesture by a lovelorn young man to his girl friend. We soon disabused them of that idea.

'More likely you'll be bought by an erring husband who's trying to convince his doubting wife that he really has ended the affair with his secretary,' remarked a severe bunch of purple irises. A dozen red roses chipped in, smugly:

'We are the flowers of true love. We are the flowers of true love. We are the flowers of true love…'

'Shut up, you are exceedingly boring!' all the other bunches called out in unison. 'And what's more, you are cheap, you have no scent and often you do not even open properly before your heads go floppy,' added a pot plant with a name none of us could pronounce.

'We are not cheap. We are not cheap. We are not cheap,' replied the roses, riled.

Eventually we decided to follow the example of the bedding plants and settle down for the night. Bickering doesn't do much for our petals, and we all knew that the biggest disgrace of all is not to be bought, and to end our lives in the dreaded green bins without having fulfilled our destiny as harbingers of joy and comfort, not forgetting our decorative qualities of course.

Early the next morning, just as the stall opened, I was proud to be the first bunch purchased. The lady said to the stall holder she liked my colours. She put me in a carrier bag, so I couldn't see where we were going. She did some more shopping after me, and it became quite crowded in the bag, what with a loaf of bread, some cat food and a plastic container of milk. She was a chatty woman and often stopped to exchange a word with passers by. Just as I was beginning to wonder if I'd make it to the end of the journey without wilting, she stopped, unlocked a door and we were home.

'Here we are again,' she remarked to no-one in particular, 'home sweet home.' She lifted me out of the bag first, and I found myself in a small, tidy kitchen, with a bunch of dead flowers on the windowsill. She took them down, poured away their water and threw them in the green bin.

'There you are,' she said to me as she trimmed my stalks and gave me some lovely fresh water in the glass vase used by the dead flowers. Constance Spry she was not, but there was plenty of room and she arranged me carefully.

My companions on the windowsill were a mixed bunch, excuse the pun! I was pleased there were no other flowers there, apart from a rather tired looking cyclamen with a few droopy blooms that needed removing. There were also three china cats, a tin opener who'd lost his way and a note for the window cleaner. I decided I was certainly top dog among that lot. The house was a big improvement after the flower stall, because I could see the television if she left the door open, and as luck would have it they were showing, yes, you've guessed it, Chelsea Flower Show!

After about three days some of me started to feel ill. The carnations were still perky but the stalk of one of the gerberers had lost its strength, and in the end she removed that one and put him in the green bin. I felt a lot better, although that particular flower had been a good sort and I did miss him. The china cats used to fight like cat and dog at night when the lady had gone up to bed. In the end two of them pushed the third one, a souvenir from Spain, off the shelf and it smashed to smithereens. The lady was very upset next morning when she found it in the sink. 'I should never have left the window open. The wind must have caught the blind and knocked poor kitty off the shelf.'

I was very lucky one day. A visitor was coming round for a cup of tea, and she moved me from the kitchen to the living room for a few hours. I was placed on the mantelpiece right in the middle, sur-rounded by little ornaments and a couple of photos. Unfortunately she had turned off the television, but the whole experience was still exciting. I learned such a lot about the neighbours: who needed to tidy up their front garden which was a disgrace, who had left his wife and then come back bold as brass two months later when his girl friend chucked him out, and who had just gone on holiday for the third time this year but couldn't afford to put a single penny in a collecting box for Save the Children.

It was just two days after that I started to feel very queasy indeed. All of me was dropping off onto the windowsill. Luckily I felt so rotten I didn't even mind when the lady came back from the shops with another bunch of flowers, and I was consigned to the final resting place, the green bin.

Alice

Another Monday morning. How often they seem to come round. Once I reached the office I soon settled down at my computer. I was designing a complicated spreadsheet which took all my attention. During the weekend I'd been mulling over a particular problem and thought I'd found a solution. I was so engrossed in it I did not notice Penny, the office manager, coming up to my desk.

'Ah Maisie, I'd like you to meet Alice. She's going to be working here for a couple of months on a special project. Alice, Maisie will show you the ropes. You know where I am if you need any help,' and with that Penny was gone.

'Hello Alice, nice to meet you. I didn't know we had anyone new starting today. Did Penny show you where everything is?' Maisie reminded me of a Stepford Wife. She was immaculate, not a blond hair out of place, smartly dressed and with a rather artificial but beautifull smile on her lips. Her eyes looked dead. Her voice matched her appearance.

'Very pleased to meet you. I start today for a period of two months. I'm working on a special project. Thank you.' She sat down at the desk next to mine and logged onto the computer immediately. Penny must already have given her the password, presumably. A bit later on I asked Alice what work she was doing but she did not reply. I wondered how she could have come into our office and started work without undergoing the induction procedure everyone went through when joining the company. Perhaps she had worked in one of the branch offices? I asked her if she had, but again no answer was the stern reply. I tackled Penny next time she walked past but just as I started speaking to her she was called away. I emailed her but when I asked her if she'd received my email she said she hadn't.

At exactly mid-day Alice left her desk, went to the water-cooler and took a long drink of water. Then she came back to her desk and resumed work.

'Alice, we are allowed an hour for lunch. Would you like to come out for a sandwich with me and a couple of other girls? It's good to get a bit of fresh air, it's quite stuffy in here, don't you think?'

'No thank you, Maisie. I must get on,' and she resumed her task on the computer. I went out with my friends as usual. Obviously I told them about Alice. We all wondered what she was actually working on. I told them I'd asked Alice and had tried to find out from Penny, but had had no success.

As the days passed I realised that none of my friends at work agreed with me about finding Alice a bit weird. I tried to explain to them how strange it was that she never ate anything at lunchtime, she spoke a bit like a robot, and she never engaged in any small talk at all. Amber, who worked in accounts, said:

'I had a long chat with Alice yesterday. It turns out she went to school with my brother. She's really nice. She's clever too, she's found a much better way of presenting the figures for our department.' That remark should have rung warning bells for me, as that was the task I was working on. But I was so surprised to find that Alice was considered normal by Amber and the others that I did not take in the significance of what Amber had said. I wondered when and where the friendly chats were happening, because I never spotted Alice leaving her desk, and most socialising after work was limited to Fridays, which it had not been yesterday.

Next day, I said to Alice:

'Amber tells me you went to school with her brother. I know Mark too, he used to be engaged to one of our friends, but they split up last Christmas.' Alice looked straight through me and then back to her work. It was quite scary. I decided the only way I could make sense of the Alice question was to ask Amber or one of the others to come into our office so that I could see how she was with them. I had forgotten to bring to the office a DVD I had promised to lend Amber, so said I would bring it to work next day and she could pop into my office to collect it. But when I reached work next morning

Alice was not there. Amber collected the DVD. When I pointed out that Alice was away, Amber replied:

'I think she's got a virus, she was complaining of a headache and a sore throat yesterday.'

Was she? How come I didn't know that? I started to feel quite paranoid. My friends had got to know Alice and found her perfectly normal. To me she was unreal, she barely spoke and when she did it sounded artificial. I never managed to see her associating with other people in the office although apparently she was friendly with some of them. Was I going mad?

When I came to work four days later, the desk Alice used to sit at had gone and so had the computer terminal she used. Penny summoned me to her office. She said there was to be some re-structuring and unfortunately the job I had been working on no longer existed. I was offered a redundancy payment and asked to leave immediately. She said she'd be happy to give me a reference when I found another job. I was shocked and upset. There had never been any bad feedbacks about my work or any critical appraisals. On my way out I saw Amber. I told her I'd lost my job and thought Alice must have had something to do with it, since she was working on the presentation of figures to the accounts department, as I was.'

'Who?' asked Amber.

Cinderella Updated

When I was at senior school my dad used to call me and my mate Owen the leaders of the pack. We was like the boss to the other kids. If we said to a kid who was scared of us or wanted to be in our gang:

'Get Sonia's dinner money,' we'd get it, no problem. Or 'Arif don't need his homework – effing teacher's pet,' and one of the other kids would grab his bag and Bob's your uncle as my dad used to say. Of course we got into trouble for bullying, detentions and that, but often we put on our 'butter wouldn't melt' faces, and got away with it. The other kids knew it wasn't safe for them to grass us up. Sometimes my dad would come raging up the school, causing what he called 'a bit of bloody mayhem.' One time he rang the local paper and made up a story about me and Owen being victimised. We even had our picture on the front page. It was wicked! He said to me 'The best form of defence is attack, son.' After that the head teacher was a bit wary of us for a while, in fact he did try to get me moved to another school but that never worked.

There was this kid in our class called Tommy Dawson. His dad's dead and his mum's a nutter. He had to collect his little sister from the child minder and he had to do the shopping and cook the tea as well. He lived in the next road to me but obviously I never had nothing to do with him. Why would I want to be seen with a loser like him? He looked like a weed, couldn't play football and you should of seen his trainers. They must have come from a charity shop. My mum said I should look out for him at school but my dad said: 'Don't be soft, it's each for himself in this world and don't you forget it.'

One day there was a special assembly. There was this geezer who used to go to our school and he started up his own business and made a load of money. But all he talked about was helping people in the community. Old folk and that. Doing things for them. He talked about duty. He said it is our duty to help them who need it. He was starting what he called a 'campaign of kindness' for the kids in our school to see who did the most for others up to the end of this school year. That was nearly two terms. And guess what the prize was? A top of the range ipad and the offer of an apprenticeship in his company when that kid left school. Everyone was really excited. Me and Owen put on a show of not caring, but when I told my dad he said he'd help me. He said the prize was in the bag.

So after that most of the kids was doing good deeds all over the place. Old folks homes was swamped with visitors. Pensioners got their gardening and shopping done. We was supposed to keep a record of what we'd done but I just made a few things up. Teachers was never going to check it all out. I didn't need to do nothing else because my dad offered to paint the village hall. Luckily enough he had a load of paint that had 'fallen off the back of a lorry.' Of course I had to go along and help for a couple of days to make it look kosher. So that was it. Sorted.

Every day I saw Tommy trailing up and down, taking an old man's dog for a walk, and someone told me he'd helped to organise a jumble sale for the nutters. But that was all small beer compared to tarting up the village hall, so I wasn't worried.

I made sure not to bunk off the day they announced the winner of the competition. There we all were in assembly. In walked Mr Moneybags. He told us how pleased he was about all the help and support so many students had provided to less fortunate local people of all ages, and a lot more eyewash as well. He said that the winner was already a credit to the school and was confident this student would in time be a valued member of their local community. He looked forward to having the winner come into his company in the school holidays to learn about his business. The winner was Tommy Dawson. I was gutted.

The End of the Affair

I never set out to have two families. Let me explain how it all came about. I'm not a bad person. But my wife Sandy, that's my ex-wife now, always said I was incapable of making decisions. I thought that was one of the reasons our marriage worked so well, because she was the bossy one and I left every decision to her. She wore the trousers, so to speak, and that suited me fine. We were a normal family with two young children, Millie and Peter. I had a job as a manager in a large company, not too far from home and everything was hunky dory, or so I thought.

But Sandy was a bit more of a go-getter than me, and as time went on she started saying that now the children were growing up we would soon need a bigger house. Or she'd point out that some of our friends were starting to buy bigger cars or go on ski-ing holidays. They all seemed to be going up in the world.

'Don't be a stick-in-the-mud, Bob,' I remember her saying. 'We want the best for our kids, don't we? More money coming in would make such a difference and there's no reason why you can't get a better job. You've got as good a chance as anyone else and you know how well you come across in interviews?' To cut a long story short, she helped me to apply for a job with a much larger salary and other perks, including a company car. I was quite happy with my old job, but, anything for a quiet life. Anyway I went for it and I got it. I can't say I wasn't proud of myself because I was, and of course Sandy was delighted. She even didn't mind that the new job involved me travelling quite a bit and not always being home at weekends.

'Don't worry about it, Bob. Me and the kids can go and see Mum and Dad when you are away at weekends. It'll all be fine.' At first the new job was daunting but quite soon I started to enjoy the challenges and was pleased I had followed Sandy's advice. Initially my trips away were just a couple of days during the week and of course it was great earning a lot more money.

As time went on the trips away became more frequent and involved longer periods away from home. Then I was sent on a project to the Scottish office of the company, based in Edinburgh. I had to spend a great deal of time up there and was given the use of a flat belonging to the company. I was not happy at being away from Sandy and the kids so much, but I was trapped. We had got used to the bigger salary and all the perks and couldn't imagine managing without them. One evening after a long chat on the phone with Sandy I went for a drink and got into conversation with a young woman, Hannah, who worked in our Scottish office too. I poured out my heart to her and she said all the right things, which Sandy had already said, about how I was helping my family to have a better life and should just get used to being away from home.

I soon settled into my work in Edinburgh, with regular trips back to the family, but Hannah became increasingly important to me. Everything about her differed from Sandy. She was a brunette, Sandy was blond. Sandy was a force of nature, Hannah was quiet and calm. Hannah was what made the time away from home bearable. I loved her for that and then of course we became lovers. We managed to keep our relationship hidden from the office. I only pretended to occupy the company flat and moved in with Hannah who owned a small cottage on the outskirts of the city. I was invigorated by my new partner, she gave me confidence and energy. I was surprised at how well I managed to keep my two lives separate. Obviously Hannah knew about Sandy and the children but when I went back home I had to be careful not to mention Hannah at all. I rehearsed a realistic account of how my free time was spent in Edinburgh for Sandy's benefit. I remembered to stress how much I missed her. It was not a lie. I did miss her. But I also loved Hannah. Luckily I never talked in my sleep. There was a tricky occasion when Sandy and the children came up to visit me. We all spent that weekend in a hotel, but I rightly guessed they'd want to see the flat which involved my moving my clothes and other possessions back from Hannah's for the duration, as well as putting food in the fridge and creating other clues

59

in order to make the place look occupied. I only remembered at the very last minute to put some toiletries in the bathroom cupboard. Peter likes looking in cupboards.

Of course with such a well paid job I was always very busy in the office and I rarely had time to stop and think about how I had got myself into such a situation. Hannah was very understanding and didn't mind when I went back south for longer periods for family holidays and half-term outings with the children. But it was too good to last. About two years into our relationship Hannah changed. Her biological clock suddenly started ticking. She wanted us to have a baby and for me to divorce Sandy. I didn't want to divorce her. It had never occurred to me to have a child with Hannah. I certainly didn't want my life to become even more complicated. We had rarely argued but now we did. With hindsight, at this point I could have gone back to Sandy, and saved my marriage. But I didn't and the next thing I knew we were expecting a baby. Of course I loved our baby, Gemma. She looked a lot like Millie, but I kept quiet about that. When I went back home the week after Gemma was born Sandy was very concerned about how tired I looked. When I went back to Hannah she spent quite a time telling me how hard it had been for her when I was away. Gemma had apparently not been sleeping at night, but once I was back she settled down again. Hannah used this as further evidence that I should come clean with Sandy and get a divorce. I could not bear the idea of having to tell Sandy what I had done. My mind was in turmoil. How on earth had I let this happen? What would I say to Millie and Peter? Who should I choose? What on earth should I do?

The decision was taken out of my hands. Fate stepped in in the form of Jean, our next door neighbour, visiting Edinburgh for the Festival. She spotted us walking along Princes Street pushing a buggy containing Gemma. She ignored Hannah.

'It is you, Bob, I wasn't sure. I see you've been busy.'

Rainbow's End

Once upon a time, in days of yore, when the world was young and witches and wizards, men and women, fairies and goblins, dragons and unicorns all roamed together freely, the very first rainbow appeared in the sky. All beings, human and otherwise, gathered to wonder at it and to speculate what it could be, where it came from and why it was there.

'We must conquer it!' cried the ogres, dismayed by the appearance of something so powerful, yet silent.

'It is magic,' declared the chief wizard, 'we should do its bidding.'

'How can we know what it wants us to do?' retorted a witch, ever practical.

'We should build a temple to worship it in,' declared a small child. Everyone was so busy making suggestions it was a few moments before they realised that the rainbow had actually vanished.

As time passed it became clear that rainbows only appeared when sunshine and rain occurred simultaneously. They showed up in different areas. They were not always complete semi-circles. The mystery of their presence occupied all living creatures for many a long day and night. Round their camp fires while they cooked and ate their evening meals they would discuss, argue and make plans on how to discover rainbows' many secrets. How did they get into the sky? Where do they go when they fade away? Who paints them? Are there, in fact, more than one?

Eventually their plans became more focussed. Unicorns claimed that since they were magic anyway it was they who would have the best chance of discovering where rainbows came from. They offered to gallop off in all directions, on a rota basis, in the hope of being in the right place when one appeared. Fairies were more scientific. They said they could sense dampness in the air because their wings became saturated, and they could therefore fly around when the sun was shining and discover any areas where rain might be about to fall at the same time. Giants and ogres obviously had a lot of influence in these discussions because even then actions spoke louder than words, and they tended to throw their weight about if ignored. They did not contribute any actual sensible ideas, perhaps because they were all men. (Just joking.) And so it went on. All groups of beings, be they winged, hoofed or human continued to rack their brains in attempts to unlock the secrets of rainbows.

Rainbows were first seen before the idea of gold as a precious metal had been established. It is not known how the idea of a pot of gold at the end of the rainbow became accepted. Suffice to say that once it became generally recognised, the search for the rainbow and, of course, its end, continued even more enthusiastically, or indeed feverishly. This may actually have been the very first manifestation of the mantra 'something for nothing.' Let us stop for a moment to appreciate the significance of that idea. 'What about stealing?' I hear you ask. But stealing is a crime. Taking the gold from rainbow's end would not, as far as we know, be a crime, it would just be good luck. Since it has not yet been discovered we do not know if that gold does belong to anyone, and if so, who?

Thus, the idea of something for nothing arose and developed and would from that day forth always be with us. People were then and still are constantly on the look-out for something for nothing. It has become the defining aim for many businesses and a vast proportion of individuals the world over. The popularity of lotteries and raffles is further evidence. It is often referred to as profit and before you interject, I am aware that buying and selling must take account of the costs of production, such as materials, labour and transport. But there are areas where profits are less straightforward to calculate. Taking a giant step forward to modern times, market forces and interest rates can be examples of what appear to be 'something for nothing.' The current ridiculously inflated property market is an example of something for nothing, commonly disguised by the term 'supply and demand.'

Going back to the early days of searching for rainbow's end, there were more serious consequences for society. Once the idea of material profit had entered the arena, the first sign of politics raised its ugly head. Creatures who had been quite happy to co-operate with different species for the greater good, started making rules and regulations to benefit themselves and their fellows and disadvantage rival species, races and tribes. One of the wizards, a natural leader and idealist, saw what was happening, and drew up a code of conduct. That idea went down like a lead balloon among some in the community who decided it did not apply to them. Sound familiar? Later, nations were formed in which the prevailing tribe or race had more power than ethnic minorities. It was not all bad. Laws were introduced which modified behaviour but the search for gold was and still is always paramount. Gold represents money and money represents power. Power comes in many shapes and sizes but there is no doubt that the lust for power is one of the defining characteristics not just of world leaders, but also of the human condition.

It is amazing to realise that hundreds of millions of people all over the world are driven by a motive which may well have developed from the fruitless search for the pot of gold at the end of the rainbow.

The Revelation

Not for the first time, I wished I had not been an only child. The sad task of clearing out my beloved parents' home, following the deaths of both my father and, nine months later, my mother, would have been, if not easier, at least less emotionally wearing had I been able to share it with a sibling. My husband Jack was coming to help the following week, but on this Saturday I had decided to take the bull by the horns, and start on the attic.

The attic had been somewhere my parents did not allow me to go alone as a child, saying there was nothing there for me and it was not a safe place to play. When I was older I had occasionally carried up boxes of items for storage, but I had never investigated what was in there. My parents were of the post-war generation that never threw anything away. So I was not surprised to find old eiderdowns, long-forgotten bedroom curtains, tired looking saucepans and even boxes of shoes, including some of my own small sandals and Wellington boots. Strange, because there was no chance of another baby in the family. I can remember begging them for a brother or sister, preferably a brother, on many occasions. In the end they had explained that sometimes mummies like mine were so lucky to have had one beautiful baby, me, but their tummies would not allow any more babies to grow there. After that I stopped asking and concentrated on my dolls.

Slowly I worked my way through the neatly organised boxes, examining the contents and trying to decide what I should do with them. There were some clothes belonging to my mother which might appeal to vintage garment seekers. Unlike me she had been a stylish dresser and despite clothes rationing had always managed to look smart and fashionable. I spent ages with a box of my old children's books. There were loads of Enid Blytons, and other favourites. I decided to keep them as I have high hopes of becoming a grandmother before too long.

My parents had kept every one of my birthday and Christmas cards and every card and letter I had ever sent them..They had kept every single school book and project showing my not particularly outstanding progress. They were all neatly labelled and boxed in chronological order. It was quite amazing. Would they have gone to all that trouble if they had had more than one child? Probably not. We had actually moved house when I was nearly eleven years old. Usually when people move they take the opportunity to have a ruthless clear-out, but my parents obviously had not done that.

I know I have made it sound as if my mother and father were mad hoarders, the sort of people whose whole house is stuffed to the brim with rubbish. But it was only in the attic that this tendency showed itself. And, as I said, it was stored in a very organised way. The rest of the house was normal: a couple of bookcases, a few ornaments on windowsills and mantelpieces, a few framed photos of family occasions, of my grandparents, and of course, precious me, but nothing out of the ordinary.

Going through all these boxes took ages, not just the weekend. When Jack arrived on the Monday he carried several boxes at a time downstairs so that I could look at their contents more easily. It was much better with Jack there. He listened to me rambling on about what I discovered and made appropriate comments. He is a very kind man. I really have been blessed with the best parents and a wonderful husband. Our daughter Lorna was married last year and she is the one I am relying on to provide grandchildren. Our son Peter is at university and so I hope he is not planning to be a father just yet, but I know he wants children too, so there was a lot to look forward to.

Getting back to the attic, another strange thing about the contents of the boxes was that there was no evidence of anything else relevant to my parents' lives having been preserved. My mother had enjoyed writing short stories and poetry, but I remember her saying not long before she died:

'Don't worry, Katy, I've thrown out all my bits of writing. You won't want them cluttering up the place.'

'That's a shame, Mum, I might have wanted to read them.'

'No, they weren't up to much. There's always the library if you want something to read.'

She had easily dismissed the efforts and achievements of her hobby. No boxes of her writings were promoted to the loft. It was the same with my father's hobby – his model railway. When he became too old to enjoy it he very sensibly disposed of it all. Some he gave to a model railway club he belonged to and some he sold. He'd loved it but did not allow sentimental attachment to stand in the way of common sense.

Jack and I were on the last lap. The attic was nearly empty. At the very back, wedged in under the sloping ceiling were four boxes. They were older and stronger than the others, and they were securely sealed with gaffer tape. Jack brought them downstairs.

'I wonder why these are taped up?' he remarked, 'none of the others were.'

'No idea,' I replied. I was actually so pleased that the mammoth task of clearing the attic was over, and that the decisions over what to recycle and what to keep had been made, that I was not interested in the final boxes. Enough was enough. I went into the kitchen to make a cup of tea. When I brought the tea back into the living room Jack was sitting with his head in his hands, looking very pale.

'Jack, are you OK?' I thought he was ill.

'Katy, these boxes are full of newspaper cuttings. I think they are about you.'

NEW BABY SNATCHED FROM HOSPITAL COT
THREE DAY OLD BABY TAKEN
BABY SUSIE – PARENTS PLEAD FOR NEWS
'PLEASE DON'T HURT MY BABY'

Baby Susie's birthday was my birthday.
Who am I?

Her Last Chance

'Wotcha doin' there, darlin',' lost yer keys?'

Greg found a blond woman, crawling around outside a shabby block of flats in the middle of the night. She was not a pretty sight. Despite the poor lighting he noticed that her jeans were filthy, and her ample girth was by no means totally embraced by the jeans.

'D'ya want some help?'

Gloria raised a tear stained face:

'The bastard's chucked me out, and now I can't find me keys. He's a drunken git.'

Gloria did not sound terribly sober herself. Greg was a kind man.

'I'll get me torch and give you a hand.'

And so began yet another episode in the life of Gloria, who, having left home at the age of thirteen to get away from her abusive stepfather, had spent years in care, and then lived with a string of what loosely might be described as 'boy friends.' One of them had taught her to drive and she had had various jobs, some of them legal. She hovered on the edge of society, known to the police and to social services but never as a case urgently needing help.

Gloria was forty years old. Her blondness came from a bottle, and a diet consisting mainly of burgers, chips and beer had not done any favours to either her figure or her complexion. But deep down she was still a homeless girl, just trying to survive and relying on a succession of men to make her feel wanted. Greg's wife had left him two years earlier and taken their son with her. She thought she deserved more excitement in her life than was available from Greg, a long-distance lorry driver. He had not been sorry to see her go, but he missed the boy.

Gloria had struck gold. Greg was a rarity in her world, a decent, caring man. He drove her to his house that fateful night and showed her to his son's bedroom where she slept like a log.

'You can stay here for a bit if you ain't got nowhere to go,' he told Gloria. She had no money and no job but he said that was fine, she could pay for her keep later.

Gloria felt safe for the first time since she was a small child. One day when she was out in the town she bumped into one of her old boy friends, Carl.

'How you doing, Gloria? You're looking good.' She told him about her new life with Greg. When Carl heard that Greg often drove to the continent he pricked up his ears.

' I might have a way your Greg could make a few quid on the side. I'll give you a bell.' Sure enough Carl rang a few days later and asked for Greg.

Greg was angry. She had put him in touch with a people smuggling racket. She had inadvertently crossed an invisible red line. He told Gloria to move out.

Stars and Stripes

My name is Stars and Stripes. Well, that's actually my pedigree name. My family just call me Stripey. I am a tom cat with unusual markings. Yes, you've guessed! I have stars on my head and stripes on my back. I am the only cat in the world known to have these markings and I am worth a lot of money. But my family loves me very much and would never sell me. They used to exhibit me at cat shows from time to time, but after a distressing incident two years ago we no longer take part in shows.

I will never forget that fateful day. There are always huge crowds of cat lovers at these shows and this one was no exception. So many people surge past the rows of cages, peering in at the cats, making comments which are sometimes quite hurtful, and then moving on. I always attracted a lot of attention, due to my unique markings. Did I tell you I am probably the only cat in the world with a coat of stars and stripes? My fur is quite short so the markings show up well. I don't know how I came to have this pattern of markings, just a fluke of nature probably.

Anyway, on the day in question I noticed a couple of dodgy looking men kept on walking past my cage, far more times than is normal. Usually you don't see people more than once, unless perhaps you hear someone saying:

'Here's the stars and stripes cat I was telling you about. Isn't he gorgeous?' or words to that effect. I'm not conceited but it is nice to get compliments about my appearance. Of course I start to purr although it can't be heard as shows are really noisy places with all sorts of announcements over the loudspeaker about judging, instructions to owners and much else. Obviously I have won a great many cups and medals over the years. My family keep them in a display case near my special bed. I don't like to boast, but I am quite a celebrity in the feline world.

As I said, these two men were hanging around my cage a lot, but strangely my family had not noticed. Then they decided to go and get some refreshments.

"Back soon Stripey, we're just getting a coffee,' and they were off. They don't usually all leave me unattended. I have my mistress – Mummy, my master – Daddy and the two children Maisie and Tom. Anyway, off they all trotted. The dodgy men lost no time. They knew my cage was firmly attached to the display bench, so one of them whipped wire cutters out of his pocket and the other stood right in front of my cage so that no-one could see what was happening. The one with wire cutters starting cutting through the front of the cage. In no time I felt myself being pulled roughly through the hole which was only just big enough, so that some of the loose wires scratched my skin. That really hurt. I had never been treated roughly before. Then I was shoved into a bag. They were wearing heavy duty gloves but I did manage to inflict a nasty scratch on the ugly face of one of them. Of course I was hissing and miaowing as loudly as I could. It was a terrible shock. The men dashed off with me, but in no time people had noticed the damaged cage and I was rescued even before they reached the car park, and returned to my frantic family.

They were mortified. They should never have left me on my own, and, as I said, they never show me now. I just stay at home and the only publicity I get is the occasional magazine interview with lots of lovely photos. I lead an idyllic life. I have fathered a few litters of kittens but none have inherited my stars and stripes. It's great being unique.

The dodgy men were prosecuted and found guilty of being cat burglars!

The Bracelet

'Mum promised it to me years ago, you must remember she said I could have it?'

'But she left me all her jewellery, Dinah. I think she knew in that way it would stay in the family, as I'm the one with daughters.' Claudia was trying to be reasonable, as she and her sister sorted through their mother's belongings. But now that their mother was gone she had decided that the era of giving in to Dinah was over. As she frequently told her own daughter Charlotte, the youngest does not have to be spoilt.

Dinah remembered transforming Barbie into a magic queen by draping round her neck the silver linked bracelet, inset with small coloured gems; and one very special occasion when Mummy had allowed her to wear it for a party when she was seven years old. It was not even 'proper' jewellery, there was no hallmark, but for some unknown reason Claudia, usually so generous, was proving surprisingly stubborn. Dinah decided to let the matter drop for a while. After all, the task at hand was upsetting enough, without falling out with her sister as well. It was strange to be emptying their mother's drawers and cupboards. Memories flooded back as blouses, dresses and skirts were discovered, some unworn for decades, still neatly folded and smelling faintly of her favourite lavender. There were boxes of all shapes and sizes containing paper bags, buttons, safety pins and elastic bands, evidence of habits learned during the war and never forgotten.

Over the weeks Claudia and Dinah gradually found homes for nearly all their mother's belongings. Of course they kept some of them. Her mammoth collection of Pyrex provided useful items for both her daughters' kitchens. Dinah took the glass chopping board with a pattern of citrus fruit, Claudia, the beautiful green fruit bowl, which had belonged to their grandmother. No more was said about the silver bracelet. Dinah was biding her time.

During the school holidays Dinah was invited to Claudia's for the weekend. Dinah's two sons were away camping with their father, an activity she had no wish to repeat after a single night's experience many years earlier.

'Bliss!" she announced to Claudia, as she arrived.

'A boy-free weekend. It was so kind of you to invite me, I've been looking forward to it all week. And I haven't seen my nieces for ages. Where are they?'

'Upstairs, playing some kind of dressing up game. They're looking forward to seeing you too. Hannah! Charlotte! Auntie Dinah is here!'

'It's good to see you without having to go through Mum's possessions at the same time. I can't believe that's all done now, and the house is actually on the market. I'm quite dreading when that's finally sold.'

'Me too,' Claudia agreed. 'The girls really miss going round there to see Grandma and playing in the garden; it's the end of an era for all of us.'

By this time Dinah and Claudia were sitting in the back garden, enjoying the sunshine. Claudia went inside to fetch some cold drinks. Dinah heard the sound of the children's voices approaching.

'Hallo Auntie Dinah, look at us!' Charlotte, in a long dress, was holding, like a train, the end of another long dress, worn by her older sister Hannah. On Hannah's curly head the silver bracelet lay balanced like a crown.

'Hannah's the queen and I'm the page girl!'

'Hallo girls! You both look very royal. I do believe you've grown since I last saw you.' As she said it Dinah realised she had made the very remark she herself used to find so annoying as a child. Then she realised something else. She did not want the silver bracelet any more. She had not missed it. The bracelet belonged with the girls. Hannah and Charlotte were carrying on its tradition.

The Grudge

I haven't spoken to my sister Peggy for forty years.

When we were small we were inseparable. We had two older brothers who were also very close. The boys mainly tolerated us and we mainly ignored them, but we all got on fine. We had a normal, happy childhood and when we were small, because we had our siblings to play with, we did not make many other close friends. Of course we had school friends but the bond between me and Peggy, who was two years older than me, was as strong as iron. She looked out for me at school and scared off any potential bullies, she made sure I ate all my lunch, she taught me how to tie a bow, she read to me when our parents were too busy. Our mother even referred to her as my other mummy.

As we grew older we both started to make other friends, and for the first time it dawned on me that Peggy did not always want me around. I complained to our mother that Peggy was shutting me out. She gave me a lecture:

'Pamela, Peggy has always been such a good sister to you, but now that you are both growing up you must understand that she is going to want friends of her own age, and you will too. You can't expect her to be your other mummy for ever.' That was a bit of a shock at first but I did reluctantly accept the truth of what she said. I still knew I was lucky to have Peggy. My friends who did not have sisters envied me, and other friends who did have them said they couldn't stand their sisters and wished they had never been born.

If Peggy sounds too good to be true it was because she was. Not only was she a perfect sister, she was also very pretty with long blond wavy hair, clear skin and perfect teeth. She had a good figure and a lovely smile. I, on the other hand, was plain. I had mouse-coloured straight hair, and a tendency to plumpness and irritability. None of that had mattered when we were small but now I was beginning to feel a little jealous of my sister. She had an ability to attract boys, and not any old boys. No, these were the desirable boys – the captain of the school rugby team, the lead singer in the school band, the boy whose parents bought him a sports car on his seventeenth birthday. She soon dropped him, luckily just before he crashed his car and was banned from driving for five years. She found that these desirable boys were not actually so desirable after all. She was too good for them.

'They have nothing interesting to say, they just want to talk about themselves,' was her correct verdict on those early conquests. Of course they also wanted to relieve her of her virginity but she was wise to all that.

Meanwhile I had made a bit of progress myself. I was now at university, training to be a doctor. Peggy was working as a personal assistant to a company director. I was lucky enough to be living at home, saving myself some of the huge debts other students were building up. I was happy and very busy, working long hours on the wards as part of my training. I had started going out with another medical student. Joe was good company and had an excellent sense of humour. It was my birthday. Joe and I, and a crowd of our friends, were meeting up for a drink in town. Unusually Peggy had nothing planned that night so I asked her to join us. Peggy had met Joe a couple of times before so they naturally started chatting in the pub. Half way through the evening I realised that Joe and Peggy were huddled together talking in a quiet alcove away from the bar. Then they rejoined the rest of us and we had a good evening, although several of us had to leave the pub early because of being on the wards early the following morning. It so happened that Joe was not on the early shift and of course Peggy did not work at weekends so Joe asked if I minded him staying out a bit longer to keep Peggy company as she did not know the rest of the crowd. You can see where this is leading. Peggy stole my boyfriend and married him.

She could have had anyone she chose, and she chose Joe. He was the sort of man she had been looking for and I found him for her. I was furious with both of them. I'm not saying that without the lure of Peggy, Joe and I would have married. Perhaps if he was so easily led astray I had a lucky escape. Nevertheless I felt betrayed, and their wedding day was the last time I spoke to my sister.

Five years ago Joe died. Peggy lives in Scotland, where she and Joe lived all their married life. I have three nephews and nieces I have never seen. I did not marry or have children. I have never forgiven her for stealing Joe. I had other boyfriends but not for long. Jealousy made me bitter and angry. Once, when their first baby was born she phoned to tell me that their baby's second name was Pamela. I put the phone down on her.

Last night Peggy phoned again. I was out. She left a message:

'Pam, how many times must I apologise? Joe is dead. I have been so hurt by your refusal to speak to me. Remember how close we were as children and ring me, please.'

The Emperor's New Clothes

Once upon a time, not so very far away and not so very long ago, two terrible wars had been waged. A great many circumstances including economic hardship, social inequality and political instability had led to the break out of armed conflict. Millions had died, some in combat, some as the result of bombing raids on civilian populations and some in concentration camps where people were incarcerated because of their religious beliefs, sexual orientation or mental health. The fighting was not confined to a single continent but spread all over the world.

In the years following, it was decided to form a union of certain adjacent countries in one continent, most of which had been heavily involved in both terrible wars. The organisation's primary aim was to allow free trade among its members, but another important intention was to prevent any recurrence of the two world wars which had engulfed so many countries in the twentieth century. Amazingly it came to pass that the organisation was formed, free trade among the member nations flourished and although fighting did still occur in parts of the continent, it was not on the massive scale of the two earlier conflagrations.

One great country was hesitant about joining the union but finally succumbed following a referendum. However it insisted on special conditions and divergencies from some of the rules followed by the other members. All countries in the union had to contribute money which was used to administer the organisation and to subsidise some of the poorer nations. In later years all except the great country agreed to use the same currency.

Eventually the bigger and most involved countries raised suggestions of a closer, federal union between members, but the great country did not wish to be involved in any such arrangements.

All member states had to agree to allow the free movement of people within the organisation. Some of the great country's citizens resented the influx of these foreigners, many of whom accepted lower wages than the local population. They blamed the foreigners for poor public services, actually due to a great country policy known as austerity; a misguided economic strategy resulting in reduced funding for all public services. Agricultural workers, health professionals, builders, lorry drivers and hospitality workers were among many categories of employees the great country relied on arriving from other union countries to make up the shortfall in both skilled and unskilled labour.

As time passed many of the advantages and benefits of belonging to the union of countries had been taken for granted by citizens of the great country. Workers rights, safety standards on drugs and medicines, student exchange arrangements, research projects, financial and banking practices, strategies to prevent criminal activity and terrorism, simple border crossing systems between member states, and ease of flights between member states were all benefits that many citizens of the great country did not appreciate emanated from the union.

Some of the most powerful politicians in the great country did not believe that membership of the union was beneficial. They campaigned over many years for the great country to leave the union, and they published articles full of lies in the press in order to influence public opinion against membership of the union.

In the end the government of the great country decided to hold another referendum to put an end, once and for all, to the question of whether or not it should remain in the union. However, there was a serious lack of information presented by those who wished to remain, accompanied by more lies promulgated by the anti-union faction. The result was that a small majority of those who bothered to vote in the referendum voted to leave. It led to a new holy grail called 'The Will of the People.'

The prospect of the great country's decision to leave the union was not a popular decision with the union leaders. Understandably they were anxious not to allow the great country to benefit from its foolish decision. It was said that the stupidity of the voters in the great country was matched only by the stupidity of voters allowing the rise to power of a racist, misogynist, shameless man child in a large country across the Atlantic. (Nobody knew then that there would soon be a lying, amoral Prime Minister in the great country too).

Negotiations to extricate the great country from the union were not an easy matter. Hundreds of officials and negotiators were hired by the great country to do the spade work, while official government representatives were selected from a very poor gene pool. The government had little idea of what it was supposed to be doing. It hoped for a settlement which would allow easy access to trade with the union, at the same time greatly reducing the number of workers from other countries coming to the great country, despite the fact that many of those workers were essential to the efficient running of the country. It turned out the great country would need to pay vast sums of money to leave the union, and it had to promise that money would be forthcoming before the union allowed any plans on future trade deals to be discussed.

The whole process was timed to last no longer than two years, but months passed during which very little progress on leaving was made. Eventually, after a great deal of climbing down by the Prime Minister, her promising to pay millions of pounds and agreeing to a fudged solution on border controls in Norther Ireland, the union pronounced itself satisfied that the first stages of the negotiations were complete and further more serious and difficult discussions on trade could start.

Most of the popular and right wing press in the great country was ecstatic. Headlines announced everything was settled and the great country was virtually free of the shackles of the union. Meanwhile informed commentators pointed out that the hardest parts of the negotiations were yet to come, that there was insufficient time left for what needed to be achieved, and there was no way the great country could have its cake and eat it regarding trade deals, those who had voted to leave declared a great victory had been achieved.

It was a classic example of the emperor's new clothes!

The Lost Memory

It seems my memory is lost
I don't know where it's gone.
It once was so reliable
But now it's just moved on.

I used to read a lot of books
And they stayed in my mind
But now I can't remember them –
My brain's been left behind.

A dismal future seems assured
Complete with shame and woe
I never thought *my* faculties
Would be the ones to go.

I don't remember people's names
Bur recognise their faces.
I try to hide my ignorance
Of those departed traces.

But sometimes they reveal a clue
Which lights a tiny flame.
I am no longer struggling
And proudly speak their name.

Alas those golden moments
Are few and far between.
More likely I'll just bluff it out
And try to stay serene

It's not as if there is a choice
Life is a lucky dip
Forgetting little odds and ends
Is nothing but a blip

Self pity's not a pretty sight
For something very minor
No-one loves a misery guts
A moaner or a whiner!

So here ends this boring dirge.
I shall put down my pen
And hereby promise not to
Mention any ills again.

The Hoofers

Giraffe walk with a gentle gait
Their necks are long and stately
They reach for leaves high in the trees
With tongues which twist sedately

But I just know behind the scenes
They learned formation dancing
In pairs performing classy acts
Which people found entrancing

Their quick-step was a piece of cake
Fast, accurate and snappy
Crowds clapped and cheered, though it was weird
And everyone was happy.

The fox-trot, with its quick, quick slow
Did take a lot of learning
But once they'd mastered steps and hold
Impressed the most discerning.

Some dances featured lifts and spins,
Quite obviously tricky.
But those giraffe, game for a laugh
Did not say they felt sicky.

Their repertoire increased each month
With dances so exotic;
The samba, jive and Charleston too
Were said to be hypnotic.

The Hoofers were the ones to watch
But guess what happened, sadly?
They missed their steps and broke their necks –
It ended very badly.

Scrabble

To place all seven tiles at once,
A triple score on letter zed,
Opponent who is just a dunce
These are the ways to get ahead.

I'm faced with o and u and i,
Exchange, but get those vowels back,
It's tricky not to moan and sigh
And glare upon the tile rack.

Then all at once the table's turned
I pick up y and k and c
And letters that I once had spurned
Bring me a score of thirty-three!

I think I have it in the bag
The end is nigh, tiles left are few
But on her very final turn
She lands a triple score with q.

There's no way now to save the game
I've lost, she's won- 'Well played!' I call.
I really need to bear in mind
Pride always comes before a fall.

Global Warming

I know that sunshine's lovely
But this is past a joke.
One careless spark on moor or park
Results in flames and smoke.

The ground is warm and solid
The plants are burnt and dead
We have been warned but leaders scorned
To act on what was said.

The subject Global Warming
Ignored for years and years,
Has gained a boost and come to roost
Exacerbating fears.

There will be droughts and famine
Migration will increase.
The world will change to something strange,
It's all beyond belief.

That Earth is overheating.
Ice-caps are melting fast.
Is it too late to change our fate?
It seems the dye is cast.

An Ongar Carol

O Little town of Chipping O
How still we see thee lie,
Beneath our deep and dreamless sleep
The traffic trundles by.
The gifts are wrapped, the savings sapped
The special day draws nigh.
How tough will be the turkey?
Will little Johnny cry?

The Christmas cards on every ledge,
The fairy on the tree,
The cupboards full of surplus food
Her Maj on BBC.
The family fights, the glitzy lights –
Greed, waste, they all belie
Eternal dreams of peace and hope –
They're sadly just a lie.

Moths, With Apologies to Wordsworth

I lay across my wooden bed
That sultry summer night of yore
When all at once above my head
A vicious, powdery moth I saw
Before the window I could close
The insect landed on my nose.

Continuous as the stars that shine
And twinkle on the milky way
More moths flew in a scary line.
A dreadful ending to my day.
They were attracted by the light
Never shall I forget my fright!

Their wings they flapped, my hands I clapped
But all to no avail alas,
I felt my energy was sapped
Then one fell in the water glass!
They must have known 'twas time to go
But how on earth I do not know.

And now when on my bed I lie
In vacant or in pensive mood
I heave a happy, hearty sigh
'Cos if or not the moths are viewed
I never leave the light to shine
Through open windows, rain or fine.

What Shall I Write?

How can I write a poem when I don't know what to say?
My mind's completely empty and has been like that all day.
I thought of writing about love and all that kind of stuff,
But those days are well past for me, of slop I've had enough.
Then I thought of Mother Nature, of fish and birds and flowers
And animals and lovely scenes folk rave about for hours.
But there again, it's all old hat, great poets got there first,
And all that I would pen would be crap writing of the worst.
What about my children and the younger generation?
To write about them is indeed a bit of a temptation.
But how to wax poetical on pigeons made of clay?
That's too much of a challenge and awaits another day!
To find a rhyme for skateboards is indeed a task too whopping,
Oh dear, now I feel the muse is drying up and stopping.
I cannot start on politics, it's much too controversial,
I'd offend too many people and would end up getting personal.
So I'll do you all a favour, cease this absurd waste of time.
You might think twice before you ask me for another rhyme!

Kubla Khan Has Another Dream.
With Apologies to Coleridge

Written before the general election of May 2015. The 'massive building plan' is imaginary, but the shortage of social housing is still with us in 2022 and shows no sign of being adequately tackled.

In Walthamstow did councillors
A massive building plan declare
Where traffic regularly ran
Through streets alive with car and van
All leading God knows where.
An area of precious land
With council homes was hopefully planned
While buy-to-letters champing at the bit
And homeless families with no place to stay
Sad victims of the bedroom tax to wit
Were praying for a miracle in May.

But oh! The uproar from the chattering classes
Who do not want the homeless in their vision.
Is this one of the country's greatest farces
As anything that's happening to the masses?
So many people victims of a system
Which means each dwelling, all accommodation
Has turned into the gold bars of the nation.
It is the currency that all do seek
Ridiculously priced, what barefaced cheek!
The economic laws – supply, demand
Have brought a shameful method to our land.
The basic human need for warmth and shelter
Is sacrificed at Mammon's famous altar.
How justify the crazy, selfish system
Which penalises people with no mortgage

Whose lives are ruined, due to housing shortage?
It is the very opposite of wisdom.
While people live in slums with mice and rats,
Cockroaches, dampness – squalid city flats.

Housing benefit – the missing link
'Tween landlords and the homeless
Does it not make you stop and think
That none of us is blameless?.
Landlords are free to raise each tenant's rent
When that is paid, then all his money's spent
The rich grow rapidly richer
Observe the bigger picture!
Unless more homes are quickly built
We all must share communal guilt.
Greed replaced our common sense
Property's become our wealth.
If building houses ran a'mok
To such a deep delight 'twould win me
Folk would get a massive shock
Council homes for all who need
Of decent size with garden space
And everyone would see them there,
A place to live without a care
With rents affordable and fair
At last a decent resting place
Where families, fathers, children, wives
Lead normal, healthy, happy lives
In homes of hope and love and grace.

Stating the Obvious

My eyes are weak, my bones are thin,
My knees are unreliable.
But for a start, I'm young at heart
Although I'm barely viable.

I try to keep up where I can
And not be moany groany.
Or try to be what I am not,
In other words – a phoney.

It's tricky for us OAPs
We're living far too long
We're blocking up the NHS
But killing us is wrong.

So we crack ancient corny jokes
And make light of our pain
And people say we're wonderful
Which goes against the grain.

'Cos we are just the same as them,
It's just that we've grown old.
We all hoped ageing could be dodged
Despite what we were told.

So get a grip, old fogies
Because there is no choice.
Of course this is not news to you,
I'm just another voice.

Ode to Pavlova or The Pudding Race

'Apple pie and treacle tart
Need more than an early start,
Step right back there Melba Peach
You are also out of reach.
Pies and puddings, know your place
You will never win this race.
Pavlova is so far ahead!'
That is what the experts said.

All deserts of every hue
Let me tell you what to do –
Move over!
We love Pavlova!

Pavlova's sweet and crunchy
Pavlova's also munchy.
Pavlova's often fruity
It is a thing of beauty.
Its taste is rich and creamy,
Its whole effect is dreamy
Pavlova, we adore you
Nobody can ignore you!

All deserts of every hue
Let me tell you what to do –
Move over!
We love Pavlova!

The House Clearance

Among the homes with doors and windows locked,
One house stands boldly, front door open wide
As council workers fling
Into a skip a lifetime's worth of everything which
Make a house a home-
A dressing table now in several bits,
The mattresses just lying on their sides,
The chairs, the rugs, the ornaments, the jugs
A box of plates and cups and knives and forks.
And much, much more…

This was Maud's home for over fifty years.
It was their home, but poor old Reg died first.
He never would give up his cigarettes.
Their children worked abroad, just Maud was left.
She had her little routines and her ways
Of filling in the hours of each long day.
With household chores and favourites on TV.
And cups of tea shared with her few old friends.

Occasionally her absent children phoned,
With tales of their careers and of their lives.
Vague promises of visits were declared, (when they could spare the time.)
They were not much concerned about her life.
And Maud was proud and never stooped to beg.

As time went on she aged, as do we all.
She found it harder doing all the work.
Sometimes she did not bother about food.
She dozed away the days.
The neighbours noticed that she was not well.
A social worker called. Her name was Gay.
Looking around Gay noticed tell-tale signs:

the washing-up left sitting in the sink,
Dead flowers drooping in a mildewed vase,
unopened post still lying on the mat.
She called another day and checked again.
The fatal words 'care home' escaped her lips.

That night Maud carefully climbed the wooden hill,
She brushed her hair and creamed her wrinkled hands.
Soundly she slept between her well-worn sheets,
When morning came she did not rise and shine,
But stayed there, rigid in her final sleep.

Soon someone else will call her house their home.
Maud's life will vanish almost without trace.
Except perhaps her garden plants will flower,
And friendly neighbours will recall her ways.

Maud's family did return to see her buried.
'Not before time' was what the locals said.
Her children left white roses on her grave.
A shame she could not smell their lingering scent.